19 Palace Gate

A NOVEL BY

JoAnn Crisp-Ellert

I held your memory
face down
under the black waves
of my rage.
I watched it sink
dry eyed
in a slow motion
tidal ballet.
From the depths you rise
like Scylia and Charibdes
grinding my bones
into a handful of dust
between the persistence
of memory and the strength
of unfulfilled dreams.

©Copyright by Bartleby

Copyright © 2004 by JoAnn Crisp-Ellert

ISBN 0-7414-1973-4

Published by:

PUBLISHING.COM

1094 New De Haven Street
Suite 100
West Conshohocken, PA 19428-2713
Info@buybooksontheweb.com
www.buybooksontheweb.com
Toll-free (877) BUY BOOK
Local Phone (610) 941-9999
Fax (610) 941-9959

Printed in the United States of America

Printed on Recycled Paper

Published May 2004

Other Works by JoAnn Crisp-Ellert

"Pablo's Search"   **1997**
Townet Press

"Pablo in Paris"   **1998**
Townet Press

"Pablo in London"   **1999**
Townet Press

**"Pablo at 3099 Q Street,
Georgetown, Washington, D.C."**   **2000**
Townet Press

"The Bauhaus and Black Mountain"   **1972**
Penn State Press

**"Henry Klumb in Puerto Rico-
Architecture at the Service of Society"1972**
Journal of the American Institute of Architecture

Dedication

Dedicated to my spouse Roberto, who has been my inspiration and constant companion through the years.

Acknowledgement

My thanks to the Royal College of Art, which provided me with studio space and an introduction to Bohemiaho, and to Abigail Welch, who acquainted me with London and its mores.

ABOUT THE AUTHOR

Stories are like leaves. Most fall heavily under the largest trees, drifting with whimsey into piles of varying size. Those piles are made more interesting by the height, width and complexity of colors which accidently interweave their patterns throughout the shadows beneath the denuded branches.

Most writers today try to weave their stories naturally through the intricacies of the combined forces of gravity and gusts of breeze.

Counter-naturalists, on the other hand, will use rakes, their feet, wind propelled machines or whatever they might, to form the pre-conceived stories that they envision.

JoAnn Crisp-Ellert, like the patient tale-weaver that she is, does not depend on nature or devices to provide her inspiration.

Rather, she takes her solid experiences from a vibrant, colorful past and creates characters that will stay in our minds forever. Images that not only entice our imagination, but will challenge us on every personal and passionate level that we could dream of or even hope to conceptualize.

There is not a character in this book that is not real to most of us, or with whom we would not love to identify. JoAnn Crisp-Ellert went straight for fundamental feelings in "19 Palace Gate."

Instead of waiting for the leaves to fall, she took a colorful reality and planted her own seeds, nurturing and guiding their growth over the years, until the leaves fell where she had pre-ordained, and the personalities were patterned after the truth of this tremulous time.

Go back, now, to post World War Two London and experience the lives and loves of people who understood exactly who they were...and could not have been otherwise.

JoAnn Crisp-Ellert is in "Who's Who in America" and has written half a dozen entertaining books prior to this novel. Educated at Syracuse University, she has studied extensively abroad in art and literature and was awarded a Post-Doctoral Fellowship at Yale University in film making.

— Holly Robert Mulkey,
book reviewer, *Current Magazine*
August 2003

Table of Contents

Chapter One 1

Chapter Two 5

Chapter Three 8

Chapter Four 14

Chapter Five...................................... 21

Chapter Six 26

Chapter Seven.................................... 31

Chapter Eight 35

Chapter Nine..................................... 40

Chapter Ten....................................... 44

Chapter Eleven................................... 49

Chapter Twelve.................................. 56

Chapter Thirteen 61

Chapter Fourteen............................... 66

Chapter Fifteen 75

Chapter Sixteen................................. 85

Chapter Seventeen 90

Chapter Eighteen............................... 93

Epilogue 98

Chapter One

The results of my real estate agent's leisurely modus operandi was Flat #2, 19 Palace Gate, Kensington, London, W8. In this flat in the proximity of Kensington Palace, which at one time was the portrait of Queen Victoria's soul, the garment of her will, I initiated my London regime. My prince consort took a carmine two-tier bus to his classes in the vicinity of Russell Square, and I began a renovation of the flat's dreary décor. We were ensconced in London! We could exult in the Dutch Gardens of Kensington Park or communicate our transgressions to the vaulted pastiche of a sodden Brompton Oratory. We could barter for aubergines in a ridiculous Soho emporium or shed plaudits on the Oliviers from the dress circle of the Stoll Theater, Chelsea. The arty denizens of King's Road were ours to imbibe.

Before this sounds like an exercise in undisciplined romanticism, I'll explain the collective "we". It is used to denote my spouse and myself, the "Lords", Gretchen and Zachary. Zach, a twenty-nine year old Professor had come abroad to pursue a Doctorate in International Law at Kings College, London University. I had come along to practice the art of dilettantism. I was already an accomplished thirty-three year old sybarite.

I didn't have the appearance Londoners ascribe to American females. I didn't have the Vogue grooming, the well-being look of "she takes complex vitamins", the Feragamo foot, or the burnished look of suburbia. Rather my lot was a square face with fatigued-looking orbs, the ubiquitous high cheekbones, unshorn tangled hair, and a Jaeger wardrobe of tweeds and cashmeres for my somewhat angular torso.

My parents were deceased and I was reared by a neurotic Aunt Stella in an atmosphere of Chippendale and Wedgwood in a hamlet in upper New York State in the Mohawk Valley. After matriculating at Syracuse University as a B.F.A. freak in painting, I fled the Baroque drawing room of my Aunt Stella; her Sunday drives in the Franklin, and her ancient retainers in outmoded uniforms. I hied myself off to a New York couturier and a Mews apartment facing Washington Square, where I knelt down and prayed five times a day facing Mecca. Several years after I arrived in the Village, I met Zach Lord. It was during my mauve and gray period. We met admiring each other's Jaguar convertibles. His was British racing green. Mine was Jaguar red. In a few weeks Zach developed a fetish for my red Jaguar and me. A judge in New York's City Hall married us. Aunt Stella was furious until she met Zach and learned he was a scion of the Boston Beacon Hill Lords, went to Harvard, and was taking me to London to pursue post-graduate studies in International Law. Incidentally, Zach's parents were equally pleased with my Aunt Stella's aristocratic lineage.

With the bilious green Jag sold, Zach, I, and the red Jaguar embarked on the "United States" and eventually, the Southampton boat train to London.

Our flat at 19 Palace Gate was on the second floor of a titanic five-story town house originally built in a flourishing British Empire by a member of the gentry. As a concession to deteriorating economics, the establishment had been divided into five one-floor maisonettes with an elevator, partial central heating, steaming hot bath water, and exorbitant rents.

Flat #2 I am sure was an afterthought by the architect to utilize some left over space. Access was gained by descending a precipitous flight of stairs. You then advanced into a long hallway topped by a monstrous skylight, fifteen feet from the floor at least, featuring a bucrane ornament in shades of verte and ochre. Off this hall to the left were a somewhat small bedchamber and a capacious studio where I could paint.

To the right and also under the high skylight was a commodious bathroom with a regal tub with claw feet that accommodated all six foot, three inches of Zach. The most significant room was at the far end of the hall. It had a cozy fireplace and a patched up hole in the wall which our charlady assured us was the result of a bomb that did not go off. She also vouched that the flat was then occupied by Edgar Wallace, the mystery writer. The kitchen beyond was a mere cubicle, the size of a small closet. Fortunately, it had a window that turned out to have a ledge, which was useful to store our lares and penates. It was also painted throughout in a melancholy, traditional, limpid stone color.

The first night we were ensconced in our eccentric flat Zach came thundering down the stairs in a magnificent mood, but then Zach was almost always in a magnificent mood.

"Well, Gretch, how did it go?"

I was sitting in the middle of a mountain of junk. I called it going through the unpacking caper.

"Gosh, Zach, I'm ecstatic! I called the Ogre (We had decided on this term of endearment for our landlord yesterday when we negotiated over a diluted sherry.) and he agreed that I could have the flat redone. At our expense, of course. Won't it be elegant not to have to look at stone colored walls. How far away from stone color can one go? I think one should go to a black wall in the hall, the drawing room in Nile green, bedrooms and bathroom, in matching light magenta, and the kitchen in bright red. We shall have an esoteric, cozy, lair."

"That's the way to go, Gretchen. The shock treatment for 19 Palace Gate and the gentry of the British Empire."

Zach gave me his dematerializing Cheshire Cat grin, exposing good teeth in a lean handsome face surmounted by unruly, dark hair graying at the temples. He then measured his six foot three cadaverous length on the dusty wall to wall carpet and dozed off.

I continued coping with my mountains of junk. Much later after a salubrious nip we strolled out into the night. I had to show Zach my cultural findings. There was a Georgian stone building where Henry James had lived, the importance added by the townhouse of Sir Winston

3

Churchill to the cobblestones of Hyde Park Gate, and the residence across the street where Millais had produced wizardry with canvas and maulstick.

When we came up High Street there was a faint light glowing in Kensington Palace. We passed the gingerbread Milestone Hotel, then by a cul de sac, and finally the gloomy and drab De Vere Hotel. We returned to a somnolent, lugubrious Palace Gate in the early hours of the morning after observing an enchanting labyrinth, a lordly Kensington, both mighty and elfin, and, certainly, without a plan.

As Zach struggled with the unwieldy portals to our building he murmured to me, "Feeling incredibly smug, aren't you, Gretchen?"

I imagine at that particular moment the answer to his interrogation would have been in the affirmative, although I never voiced it.

Chapter Two

The next month was a pregnant one. I was surrounded by my black wall, Nile green drawing room, magenta bedrooms, and a bright red kitchen. Liberty of London supplied contemporary furniture, Chelsea Pottery a tile bar, and Harrod's a flower barrow. My abstract, multicolored, paintings were hung throughout the flat. None of this ambience was compatible with the English notion of décor. Consequently, they viewed it as a matter of great curiosity and a certain amount of angst.

But by far the most salient event of my sojourn to date was Petronella!

Petronella Adams, an American ex-patriot and a dedicated Anglophile, was an opulent friend of an opulent friend of mine in Georgetown, and also a friend of Aunt Stella's. Our initial encounter with Petronella was classic.

We drove up in front of 7 Pelham Crescent at twilight on a crisp December day.

"Aren't you glad you wore your dark-blue, pinstripe Brooks Brothers suit?" I asked Zach as he climbed out of the Jaguar. He ignored my interpolation.

"Quite a mausoleum she has," he said, studying the four story Georgian building. "Shall we genuflect twice, Gretchen?"

"Don't be difficult, darling. See if you can find the doorbell."

As Zach searched for this elusive item, the door swung open. We were greeted by a corpulent, but well-groomed maid, who announced that madam would receive us in the drawing room.

As we followed her undulating posterior, an agile glance at the hall and two adjacent rooms convinced me that the home had been furnished in a lavish but somewhat haphazard manner. When we entered the drawing room I discerned that Petronella had married Victoriana and Queen

Ann and it was working well.

Petronella, herself, was reclining on a cerise Victorian chaise lounge and wore a frock analogous in hue to the chaise. She half rose to greet us and I surmised that she was about five feet tall. Truly, a mischievous sprite presiding over this colossal drawing room. It was all wrong. She was out of proportion with the Adams' fireplace, the clavichord, and the Queen Anne table. Her long physiognomy was hideously attractive. Two porcine orbs, a generous proboscis, and two lines sentineled a slight gash of a mouth. Petronella had celebrated forty plus natal days.

Glancing through a lorgnette she trilled, "The Lords! Ever since Stella wrote about you I've been waiting to meet such clever people."

I observed thereafter that the lorgnette appeared only at events such as the Saddler Wells Ballet and the Royal Academy Exhibits.

Hurriedly she continued her monologue. "Do sit down," indicating two unstable looking antiques with a bejeweled hand. "We're going to have great fun, Gretchen and Zachary. May I call you Gretchen and Zachary?"

Then not waiting for an answer, "Tell me, you two, was the trip over beastly? It always is unless you travel first class on the 'Liz'. Where did you say you are lodging? I do hope Kensington. Some parts of London are quite dull, but not Kensington."

At this point there was enough of a dramatic pause for me to retort.

"Yes, Petronella, we have managed to locate a flat on Palace Gate opposite Kensington Gardens."

"How nice! You should be quite comfortable there with the Duchess of Kent as a neighbor. I must have you invited to the Palace. The only trouble might come in the summer. Tourists, you know, love the area. They come from the De Vere Hotel and the Kensington Palace Hotel. Americans mainly, who ask inane questions, can't articulate, and wear odd looking costumes..." She chuckled slightly at her own wit.

"Zachary, be an absolute dear, and pour us a sherry from that amusing decanter on the marble table. Isn't it a divine shape? Belonged to one of the Sitwells."

Zach obliged, and I had a moment to study Petronella in repose, a state in which one rarely found her. When we each had our tawny potions, we did the customary "Cheers" and Petronella resumed her loquacity, adroitly. I believed the ring mistress would always have a well-directed circus.

Chapter Three

An engraved invitation arrived on December 12th inviting us to a Holiday soirée to be held by Petronella Sybil Adams at 7 Pelham Crescent, Belgravia on December 24th at 8 p.m.

When we arrived festivities had already started. As we were announced I perceived that Petronella's eyebrows ascended ever so slightly. We, oh, unpunctual Americans, the last to arrive. The halls and rooms were decked bountifully with boughs of evergreen. A singularly handsome silver Christmas tree (which I recognized as a by-product of Harrod's) stood in the drawing room towering over the heads of Petronella's coterie. There was an elaborate crèche beneath the tree.

Petronella, attired in seasonal spruce green velvet, rushed to greet us. After introducing us to all, she deposited me with the most formidable appearing gentleman in the group, a six foot Adonis who had reached mid-life and who had an obvious Saville Row tailor.

"This, my dear, is Tony Carmichael, I want you to become especially good friends. Tony is the most magnificent person in London, but he won't stay here for long. He has interests in Africa and is always popping off to the Belgian Congo. There he becomes the most magnificent person in all of Africa." And with that Petronella was off to apportion her other guests.

"She is quite right, you know," said Tony in a cultivated, resonant voice.

"Right about what?" I asked cautiously.

"About my being the most magnificent person in Africa. You see, there's no one left in Africa these days other than the natives. Everyone is going to the States. I'm going to become a capitalist myself by going to the States. Am I treading on your extremities? But Gretchen, there's no denying it, you are a capitalist. You're wearing a George

Jensen bracelet."

"The bracelet is merely a stage prop. It's out on loan for the evening. Don't let it influence your evaluation. I am really an artist. Tony, let's talk about Africa. Has Cairo changed much since I was there some years ago? I've heard that Europe is getting to be an over-run antique shop. But Africa, well, Africa goes on as Hemingway predicted."

"You're quite right about Africa, and Europe too, for that matter. I suppose, physically the greatest change in Cairo in the past few years was the destruction of Shepheard's Hotel by that damned conflagration."

"Will the new Shepheard's be an architectural triumph? It's going up near the Seimiramis, too, isn't it?"

"Gretchen, at the rate the new Shepheard's is going up, none of us will be around to see it. Ah! But it doesn't affect my life-style one bit. Dirty Sam, the bartender for the non-existent Shepheard's, after the fire picked up his accoutrements and moved next door to the Seimiramis Hotel. He makes just as fine a Suffering Bastard cocktail as he did at Shepheard's, even more potent.

"Yes, I've heard about those Suffering Bastards. You must be very strong to drink them Tony. Did you complete the ceremony with full marks so you could imbibe his sequel, the Dead Bastard?"

"As you may know I am terribly boastful. I actually got to the final stage, the Resurrecting Bastard."

"Did someone mention my name in vain?"

Turning, I saw sauntering up to us a short figure whose jauntily hung lounge suit expressed youth, an impression immediately neutralized by an obvious rotundity at the waist and a visage reflecting the first vestiges of hedonism.

"Have you met my partner Ian Richards, Gretchen?" Tony asked.

"I think he was indulging in the wassail bowl, when I was being introduced around," I retorted.

"Ian, this is Gretchen Lord, so far she is one of my favorite Americans. Terribly artistic, for an American, that

9

is."

Ian spoke in clipped tones. "So nice to know you Gretchen. We must talk about what London has to offer while you are with us. Tony, Petronella is panicking. She says she needs the help of your black magic with the egg nog."

Tony took his leave, urbanely.

Ian continued, "If you are going to pursue your art here, I think the only place is the Royal College of Art. Normally one applies through channels and it takes eons to be admitted, but if you know someone on the Board there are ways of being admitted quickly. Of course the Slade has a name as an art school and also St. Martins, but the Slade hasn't been the same since Johns left, Augustus Johns, I mean."

"Yes, I know whom you mean without providing me with the full appellation, Ian."

"Good, I see you speak our language then and know about the Slade. However, I must exhort you to consider the Royal College. If you do, call Tony, he has connections there."

While Ian exhorted, a young woman in a blue dress draped over a meager frame, announced that the festive board awaited and groups gradually dispersed to invade the dining room.

The festive board was resplendent with exotic preparations. I learned subsequently that Petronella did most of her traveling via her cookbook. There was Boeuf Burgoyne, Asparagus Au Gratin, Rum Wafers, French Salad, Pate de Fois Grás, Caviar, Fruit Salad with Kirsch ā la Fortnum Mason. In short, a hunt board covered with a magnificent buffet. To replenish the dishes, Petronella kept calling a servant with a silver handled instrument with clattering prongs. She explained this was her Georgian baby rattle. "Antiques can be so utilitarian!"

During the buffet, I was casually engaged in conversation with a young English writer from Liverpool and his, well, let's call her his "friend." The writer,

Woodrow Birley, seemed a bit ordinary and mesocephalic. I never did ascertain quite what his features were as Petronella had lit the dining room totally with tapers. The effect was wonderfully macabre, but discouraging to perception.

Woodrow said glibly that he was prostituting his talents writing "thrillers" in Liverpool, when he was really destined to write poetry in Capri. As we chatted, I glanced laterally at Zach and winked as he was discussing foreign affairs with a youthful silver-headed siren.

Irish coffee was served with Gregorian chants in the drawing room. At this time, a rather drunk and dynamic character by the name of Lawrence D'Arcy made his full impact. The chants had been in process for ten minutes and serenity prevailed, broken only occasionally by a subterranean whisper.

Larry came clattering into the drawing room, surveyed the tableau, and observed distinctly: "Mesdames and Messieurs, isn't it a real good thing that they've discontinued these monotonous Gregorian chants in the churches?"

A dramatic pause ensued.

Tony rose to the occasion. "Larry, you must have had a strenuous journey. From where did you say you just returned?"

"Back from India, by way of South Africa." Larry said this swaying slightly. "I had a terrible malady and they wanted to put me in a lazaretto, but my medico decided I wouldn't have to wear the Lepers Bell, after all." With that Larry collapsed on the Victorian sofa.

Needless to say the Gregorian chants had desisted and general conversation resumed.

She of the blue dress and meager torso, Matilda by name, supplied me with a fill-in on Larry D'Arcy. He was not, as one might expect from his accent and mannerisms, French. Rather, he was an American hailing from Boston and, of course, Harvard. He owned a share in a lesser known Greek shipping line. The where-with-all from this venture enabled him to maintain a thirteen room flat in the Albert

11

Mansions, a Bentley, and a dusk to dawn existence which paid little regard to office hours. Larry was attractive with sure, strong, middling limbs, meant to move gracefully at cocktail parties and on the dance floor. When sober, his dark, handsome face and genteel manners were an asset to his host. Unattached and twenty-eight, Larry was wonderful for unescorted women, early in the evening, that is.

Shortly after Larry's collapse, Petronella announced that we were invited to Tony's flat which was also in Belgravia and just a few streets away.

Tony's flat in Belgravia, it was truly the pièce de resistance of the evening. A majestic Regency home, which was owned by Tony, housed his ground floor flat. The upper three floors were divided into maisonettes which he rented to senior diplomats and the bowels of the edifice were inhabited by a caretaker couple. The group arrived in various types of transport, including taxis. Zach and I, however, were transferred, somewhat erratically, by the now revived Larry in the aforementioned Bentley.

As we entered the flat I heard two middle-aged "girls" gasping in concert. The initial introduction to Tony's drawing room produced that sort of effect on most people. I then heard Tony's low cultural tones reciting so it was audible to most of us.

"I suppose this room is quite good, but I'm not entirely satisfied. I was in Africa when it was redone, and I don't whole-heartedly approve of the marbleized effect the decorators used on the wall nor the two Nubian statues Ian picked up. How could you have done it, Ian? They have to go!" Tony continued on. He was the impeccable image of the landed gentry condescending to show the oafs about.

Zach was pouring himself an after dinner brandy from the sideboard and I took the opportunity to study the room leisurely. It was theatrically attractive: an enormous drawing room with an aqueous blue ceiling, marbleized walls, a white and black marble Adams fireplace, flanked by two oversized black velvet settees, two black marble tables supported on two carved white eagles, the two life size

Nubian statues, gilded candelabras, a 3'x6' painting of a youthful Tony, and a purple Oriental rug. The entire wall on the left side of the room as one entered and faced the fireplace was encased by the most wonderful library. A now sober, Larry showed me that by pushing a panel an open sesame was performed, giving access to the music room. According to Larry, the music room was Ian's sanctum sanctorum where he played the grand piano it contained beautifully. This was a striped, black and white wallpaper room with dubonnet velvet chairs and a thick Persian rose rug. Petronella then gave us a duplex choice: dancing in the drawing room or listening to Ian play in the music room. I mused, a well-run circus must have an agenda.

I decided to go along into the music room with a young English doctor and his Australian wife. After a few of Ian's conservative compositions we became a bit obstreperous and started to sing songs like "Oh Sir Jeffre." During the third stanza, when I had just learned how to cope with the chorus, Tony surreptitiously bore down on Ian.

"I say, Ian, do you have to play that type of thing? Dreadfully ribald, you know. Why don't you come out to the other room and mazurka with the rest of us?"

He gave Ian a playful clap on the shoulder blade and the musical was over.

Zach and I left shortly after this incident. In a hallway, as opaque as night and aglitter with gold, I can still hear Tony as we commended him on his flat. Waving an arm to indicate his exotic surroundings, "All this is not difficult for me, you know. I have an instinct for it."

We left him on center stage.

Yes, Zach and I thought, these are two strange men.

Heterosexual? Inverts? Mountebanks? The ingredients are unknown as yet. An experiment in the chemistry of human nature. And those who knew the answers, acted smugly, and divulged neither by mot or action what they knew.

Chapter Four

Boxing Day loomed over us two days later and the prospect of a cocktail party at Larry's. After presenting Yuletide tokens to our caretaker, Mrs. Tattersall, which as near as I can estimate is what makes Boxing Day in London, we went along to Larry's. His thirteen rooms in the Albert Mansions were boiling with guests greeting each other with "Happy Boxing Day!" With a modicum of sobriety Larry presided effectively over his Louis Quinze drawing room. Zach and I observed that Tony and Ian were not among the beautiful people present. Petronella was there, of course, acting as Larry's surrogate by introducing guests and helping Mrs. Lambert, his housekeeper, serve a cold buffet. We met the other half of Larry's Greek shipping line, George Zacharias, a short, dapper, mustached gentleman who smiled genially and offered us an Ouzo. As we sipped the milky liquid we discussed how Britain had pilfered the Elgin marbles and installed them in the British Museum. Proffering our condolences, we surreptitiously left "Happy Boxing Day" to view the nearby Albert Memorial, in the moonlight; in the lovely moonlight.

I walked through the remainder of the holidays with the aesthetic. I drank Gordon's Gin with the aesthetic. When I interrogated the aesthetic regarding art study, the inevitable reply was the Royal College of Art.

After the holiday season I contacted Tony and told him about my conversation with Ian about London Art Schools. Tony said Ian had told him about my interest and that he expected me to call him when I had decided. I told him my choice was the Royal College. Tony congratulated me and said he would arrange an appointment with his friend, Professor Rodney Sanders, who was the head of the painting department.

The day of my appointment at the Royal College, which was then located on the top floor of the Victoria and

Albert, proved pluvious and frigid. Zach had the Jaguar, so I stood in the queue at Palace Gate waiting for the No. 49 bus, cowled in black, with a matching portfolio. Rodney had wanted to ogle some of my work.

The other faces in the queue were English faces, grim and intent faces, half beclouded by umbrellas. I didn't envy them for their damp cradle to the crypt existence. I did envy them their weather boots and heavy rain gear. Items I must soon indulge in. I mused to myself, go to Aquascutumn at the first opportunity. I should have called a cab. There was a slight undulation in the queue. I looked in the direction of the De Vere Hotel as the carmine, double-decker bus showed itself around the corner making the only splash of color on an otherwise drab Kensington High Street. The bus halted noisily. A cockney voice called out, "Let 'em off first, Guv." His exhortation was directed to an elderly gentleman, first in the queue, who flourished a long handled umbrella trying to get admittance. The bus disgorged a nanny with two toothsome, wailing juveniles, and swallowed our queue to distribute it to Hyde Park, Mayfair and Oxford Circle.

By the time the bus deposited me near the Victoria and Albert Museum only a fine rain was falling as I maneuvered the remaining few blocks without dire incident. The Royal College was located on the third floor of the V&A. My entrance to the altar of aestheticism was dimmed as the lift ceased operating between the second and third floors. I had pushed a button at random and this was the result. In response to my agitated, "I say I'm stuck" cries, I was rather unceremoniously bailed out by Professor Sanders' secretary.

Rodney Sanders, somewhat smallish with a large globular head and scholarly spectacles was in the hallway shaking with mirth.

"Don't they have lifts in America, Miss Lord?" he asked. He persisted in calling me Miss Lord even after he met Zach.

I rallied to the occasion, "No sir, we only have elevators," and followed in his wake.

It was a very leisurely appointment. We talked about the liberal arts, the useful arts, and eventually got around to the fine arts. While we conversed Rodney Sanders kept doing things with what seemed to be a paper weight on his desk, picking it up and putting it from side to side with neurotic movements. Every now and then he would panther back and forth in the small cubicle that served as his office or glance abstractedly at a pastoral painting by Samuel Palmer on the wall. He finally gathered himself together and spoke sententiously and at length about the complications of art in the nineteenth century and how difficult it was to explain its development.

Someone had entered the office quietly, someone emanating a pungent odor of turpentine and oil. We turned simultaneously to inspect the interloper. The interloper was masculine, six foot, three and was hovering in the doorway.

"Derek, so glad you came along. The girl I was telling you about is here." Then to me, "Miss Lord, this is Derek Townsend, our youngest Assistant Professor. As I've accepted you as a special student, I've assigned him as your tutor. Why don't you take her about, Derek, and show her the apprentices at their easels?"

Derek wore an amused, listening face, "Yes, that would be a good thing. Do come along." His low voice was tinged with Yorkshire. As he deposited an unfinished canvas in the corner of the office, I noticed his gray suit. It was cut rather in the Edwardian style prevalent amongst artists, no shoulder padding, full skirt on the jacket, high lapels, tapered trousers et al. A commingling of Bohemiaho and Edwardianism, superintended by a Victorian.

Rodney smiled at me with an *Ita mitte est* look as we departed.

When we went into the first studio for inspection his eyes came to hazel light as we passed under the skylight. Derek was young, twenty-one perhaps, talented perhaps, and handsome in a more virile way than most painting instructors who had crossed my existence. He was clean shaven when I first knew him. I noticed his physiognomy: small, constantly

16

observant orbs, a few riptides in his hairline, rectilinear nose, munificent smile, a longer growth of hair than most American males I was accustomed to.

"I say, Miss Lord I don't know that I am the best candidate for this assignment."

I had gone over to the other side of the vacant studio to inspect some of the students' efforts. I turned, and walked deliberately back to face him.

"Derek, we have been incorrectly introduced, the name is Mrs. Lord. But aren't most of the students here on a first name basis?"

"Yes."

"Then, my Christian name is Gretchen."

"Well, Gretchen, as I was saying, I'm sort of a square peg in a round hole here. 'Non Serviam' and all that sort of thing. I'm not in accord with the regime. I have no friends, only accomplices. I'm seeking another appointment and should be leaving come June, I believe the students come here out of imbecility or mythomania."

"You're absolutely right about me, I belong in both categories. I am so glad we have factions here. I adore big academic messes."

"Don't take me so literally. I just want you to understand my position."

He said this, obviously never taking his absorbed eyes from my countenance. I thought he knew my bony structure so well in fifteen minutes that if I turned around he could do a detailed sketch. Obviously, well-trained, not the country club fine artists I had known at Syracuse University. The artists of answering roll-call at 1pm and roaring off to Drumlins to drink beer. Later the Phi Delta party at their big house at the end of Walnut Avenue where umbilical cords were checked and prospective seduction prowled on ocelot feet. And the Fine Arts consisted of wearing four fraternity pins even in the shower. I know I'll marry and don't have to go to the damn life classes because one of these fraternity pins will take care of me for the rest of my unnatural life. Einee, minee, mine mo, yes here was an easel artist. I was a cocktail artist. I talked a good game.

"Have you met Cracknell?"

I must have looked nonplused as he continued.

"He is our High Llama, only appears after tea time.

Yes, the President of this institution has been a-grailing. Just got himself a Knighthood last year and a Rolls this year to go with it. They're a set."

"How nice! I am meeting one of the original Angry Young Men."

He laughed congenially, "You know, Gretchen we have some of the greats. I mean internationally recognized ones on the faculty here. It's incredible what politics and the course ahead of you running in orderly furrows to the Royal Academy will do. I'm on overflow today. The complex sentences just keep coming."

"If you're not going to show me the apprentices at their easels, I expect I'd better be leaving."

"Sorry about that, but Wednesday afternoon is serene here. Saunders forgot that as he often does."

Derek had a habit of teetering back and forth on his long limbs, he did this now still studying me. By this time there must be the latent framework for a portrait.

"Life class is scheduled Monday at 9am, but don't be too punctual, the models never arrive on time. One of my pet peeves," he said bitterly. "No one is too assiduous here."

"An innovation," I countered. "Life class without Life."

I then proceeded to make my descent by staircase rather than the lift.

When I reached the flat, Zach had already returned from Kings College and was clinking ice cubes and glasses in the kitchen. He came to the doorway of the hall, holding our hammered, aluminum, cocktail shaker firmly. As he looked at me, a bemused expression crossed his face.

"What's all the impedimenta? Gretch?" indicating the portfolio with a nod of his head. "Are you going to hang in the Tate?"

"Don't be an ass, you knew I had that beastly

18

appointment at the Royal College today."

"How did it go?"

"Beastly, what sort of potion are you concocting in that thing?"

"Darling, I am concocting a brace of martinis and afterward you and I are dining at the Chelsea Pensioner, a little place Bradley Peyton the Third recomended."

Bradley Peyton the Third was one of our compatriots also studying at Kings College and a new friend of Zach's. I had not as yet met Bradley Peyton, whom I understood was a confirmed Anglophile, but I was anticipating the encounter.

"If Bradley Peyton the Third recommended it, it must be very, very English," I replied, heading in the direction of the bathroom to draw water and share our king size bath tub.

Located on Lincoln Street, just off King's Road in Chelsea, it was a typical little restaurant replete with artists and atmosphere. I understand it is still there only they now call it Au Pere Nicole. It has been expanded, it isn't so typical anymore, and Laura isn't there anymore. But I didn't describe Laura! I must tell you. Laura was a parrot. A parrot who had attained the remarkable age of 105 years when I first saw her. She had a lovely shape with variegated feathers and was inclined to be a little saucy. She ogled us with a disenchanted orb as we munched our eight shilling, six, dinner. Midway Zach suddenly looked up as if he had remembered something.

"Gretchen, you know why this place is called the Chelsea Pensioner, don't you?"

"No, I must confess, oh learned one, I don't. However I can't count on an oracle like Bradley Peyton the Third as one of my acquaintances."

"Well, you've seen these hale and hearty old men in their red tunics trundling down King's Road and frequenting the local pubs. They are retired English soldiers and their habitat is here in Chelsea."

"Isn't this volé au vent good?"

"Gretch, have you been listening to anything I've been saying?"

19

"Yes, dear, only I want to see where Oscar Wilde lived in Chelsea before I start my survey of the Chelsea pensioners."

Then thinking I might have offended him, I reached over and put my cold handle extremity on his, "Aren't you glad we ate out tonight?"

I didn't know that I was unhappy then. Maybe Laura sensed it. At least only Laura would know that six months from now a different Gretchen with a different man would be entrenched at the same table.

Chapter Five

Zach was extremely preoccupied with his International Law classes at King's College. He always claimed that we fine art majors never had to read books, while he had to spend hour upon hour exploring entire libraries. Consequently, I was glad when Monday morning arrived. I had decided to do Life Drawing twice a week on Mondays and Fridays. A critique of my work by my tutor, Derek, was scheduled for Wednesday. At that time I was to receive some fundamentals in portraiture, as well.

Cultivating a demeanor of being casual and not anxious about the Monday program, I appeared in the studio a little late. A bovine model was posing. All the best situated easels were taken, industry was omnipresent. There was a brooding quietness, broken only by the sound of charcoal scratching and the buzzing of a small, electric fire. The chill air seemed full of creative genius. I was ignored. How dare I intrude? They had all been to Parnassus. Derek was nowhere to be seen. Was there no one in command? I stood in the frigid room surveying, with mounting apprehension, the artistic pantomime of dedicated artists, working feverishly. Not for me, I had not come here to be a slave to the palette.

After a few minutes the serenity was broken by staccato male tones which emitted from an easel across the room.

"All right, break time, be back in fifteen minutes and we'll continue this pose."

Evidently, the don worked along with the apprentices in this class. It was a mixed bag of about twenty-five males and females dispersed on trousered limbs, surmounted by flamboyant jumpers, and pinnacled by weird hairstyles. I assumed they were headed for the common room and their beloved cup of tea. The instructor headed for me.

As his suave, middle-aged composure moved toward me, I thought, here is someone whose aspect fulfills the romantic concept of a painter.

"It is Mrs. Gretchen Lord, is it not?" he said muttering the interrogation slightly in his magnificent dark beard. "The name is Mansfield."

"Very nice to meet you Professor Mansfield. I must apologize for my tardiness this morning. It won't occur again."

"Don't worry about it. Good to have you with us. Spent some times in the States myself in 1939. Went out to Mexico for a year just to paint wonderful country. Like to go back."

He spoke quite disjointedly. It impressed me after I had known him awhile how his imagination was continually abstracting him.

"Excuse me for now, have to go along and have elevenses with Saunders.Standing appointment and all that."

Taking a brier pipe out of his corduroy jacket pocket, he sauntered out of the studio. Within a few seconds his well formed hirsute skull appeared again in the doorway.

"Oh, Mrs. Lord, if there's not an available easel when the students return, live dangerously, go out and filch one from another studio." With a wink of his mischievous left eye, he was off again.

In fifteen minutes the model was back and a few students began dribbling by me, taking their places rather indolently at their Strathmore paper. Someone called "Time" and the model cooperated by removing her robe and resuming her pose. I noticed she was now in front of the electric fire.

As time lapsed some easels remained vacant. The same degree of industry that walked through the portals at the first break never returned, at least on that particular day. As Derek had intimated there was indeed a policy of laissez-faire here. I found an easel and started to draw.

At noon, Derek appeared and took me to the common room where we had a simple lunch and an elaborate conversation about nothing.

I imagined I had put my child's toys away nine years

ago when I left the University. Now I had gotten them out again, I thought, as I sat fortified with my vine charcoal, Strathmore paper and fishing tackle box at the Royal College week after week doing life drawings. Derek's presence when I was at the drawing board was a menace to my security. I was always glad when he made some glib remark like, "Gretchen, that model is robust enough to be all right for Reubens."

One day he suggested strap-hanging on the tube to one of the Tate exhibits. The wonder and magic of the Pantheon-like Tate Gallery: Sargent speaks to you eloquently and tacitly, Picasso shouts harmoniously, and Soulange, perhaps, frightens you a bit with his brutal brush strokes. I have always been intimidated by the Tate and probably will continue to be.

On our second junket to the Tate, Derek suggested that we have tea in the Whistler room. He had brought his usual overflow of conversation along with him.

"Well, aren't we just like those South Kensington dowagers, having tea in the Whistler Room, ogling the murals before we climb into our limousine."

"Derek, I thought Wednesdays weren't going to be your bitter days any more?"

"India or China tea?"

"India, please."

"You'd prefer to discuss the Sutherland portrait of Maugham?"

"Yes. Aside from that unfortunate palm leaf, what do you think of it?"

"I think this. Like most of Sutherland's portraits it is more of a caricature of the subject."

"But the color? Don't you think it works quite well? I know. I know. There's no place in your life for contemporary art. Why don't you grow a beard and wear a cloak?"

"Why? To prove to myself that I'm out of the pubic stage?"

"Don't be nasty."

23

"Would you still have tea with me and my beard?"

"Of course. But what about Sarah?" Sarah was his sometime girlfriend, a nebulous form that remained nebulous for quite some time.

"I do believe she loathes beards. Anyway, Sarah is soon going to the States on an art grant."

And then we were off on protracted divagations: a murder in the tube at Glouster Road, the Diaghliev exhibit at Forbes House, the new Mercedes 300, and a patriarch dying in his consort's council flat. But mostly Derek talked of Yorkshire. When he spoke of his hallowed land, his obeisance filled the room, and his magnificent eyes had added luster. I was a good listener. I was beginning to know Yorkshire vicariously.

Leeds, Bradford, Keighly, Bingly and Bronteland were an integral part of Derek's particular skein of life. However, his childhood was a story of marginal existence and parental inadequacy, adumbrated by the war.

How did he phrase it one day? We were sitting on a hard, blanched, stone bench in Holland Park. The model had not shown up for portraiture class, so we had nipped along to dissect an open air sculpture exhibit. We were sitting near an ample Henry Moore and a spindly Reg Butler production, neither of which pleased Derek.

"You're the issue of wealthy parents, Gretchen. I'm a serf, a pauper, a swine, of, and from the earth. You tell me I can easily sever the shackles of my environment. I disagree. Yes, you can sit there smugly in your cashmere coat worrying whether you can have another Jag, because Zach uses yours too much. You're incredible. If you're born a serf, you stay a serf, takes gold to make gold."

"Derek, you should give daily thanks to Zoroaster or whom ever you pray to, for your talent."

"Anyone can paint, girl. It's just hard labor! Oh, I give thanks to my particular icons all right. I give thanks to the salaciousness that crawled through the serf blood of my accursed ancesters. I give thanks for the dismal cell in which I was born while a squalid midwife bandaged my naval. I give thanks for every flailing I had as a boy along with the hours of family indifference and older brotherly curses. I give thanks for the ten minutes of free advice that sent me off gloriously to art school in Leeds at the age of thirteen. For twelve years I've been trying to find my way out of this damned web, to get some beauty in my life. I think it will be a lifetime project." He smiled faintly at this last remark, and a crimson color that had risen to his lean face began to subside.

Several times I had attempted to cut this outburst short, but to no avail. Now that he had finished, I was stymied. I felt my tear ducts doing strange things, so I sat silently for a few minutes studying the huge Henry Moore woman in stone. Then, again trying to change his mood, I got up and removed my cashmere coat, and flourished it with all the aplomb of a matador.

"Earmark of a capitalistic society, I shall wear you no more. I don't like the speeches you provoke. You are banished to the land of lost coats. Zach grumbles when I'm late for cocktails. Shall we leave?"

There was no where else for our conversation to go. Yes, it was in Holland Park that I first realized the true fathom of Derek's bitterness.

We walked to the Odeon at the juncture of Earls Court and Kensington and caught my favorite No. 49 bus.

Chapter Six

Kensington Gardens, and the immutable Kensington Palace, prepared to receive Spring. Cumulus clouds furnished a backdrop for kites, fashioned in non-objective shapes. The Dutch Gardens bloomed gloriously. The scene was appraised by the char with the brown paper bag marked Barkers, and the old man sunning himself on a bench and peering from behind the London Times. Prams with hygienic-looking cherubs propelled by efficient looking nannies pursued by trim toddlers, appeared in legion. The Albert Memorial with burnished tones looked down upon a small queue purchasing tickets for a London Symphony concert at Albert Hall. And I? Like the coming of Spring, I was undergoing a metamorphosis, too. I can't relate its different stages. They were never too lucid. It even occured to me on several occasions that I must oppose this permutation.

Derek was the stimulus for this metamorphism: gaunt Derek, with the brooding façade, the miraculous paint brush, and the disheveled hair. Initially, I told myself, this is a false affinity, a fixation, the desire to possess a like mastery over canvas. I was very objective. I was Gretchen Lord. I never became emotionally involved, not even with Zach. I had married him for better, not for worse. We were of the same class and looked well together. Our proportions were right. His dark complexion complimented my blondish hair. We liked the same type of sports cars. But did I love him?

As I mulled over the dragons threatening my comfortable and benign life style, I had the occasion to meet Sarah.

It was a night in April, the central heat consisting of two small radiators had been turned off, and I was complaining about the polar conditions. In London we refer to the calendar and not to the climatic conditions when cutting off the heat. Zach had fallen asleep in the green

Hardoy chair, rather an unusual feat considering its butterfly shape. At his side, face down on the wall-to-wall carpet, lay a formidable looking book with a cover that said International Law. The BBC announced over the wireless that it was 8pm and our telephone rang. Having by now learned the proper response, I answered.

"Kensington 1778."

I could hear pennies going awkwardly into the slot of a kiosk somewhere in London and then Derek's voice.

"Gretchen?"

"Yes, speaking."

"Derek, here. I say, do you mind if Sarah and I drop in on you tonight? Sarah wants to talk to you about her art grant."

"It's not an awfully good night for us, Derek. Zach has a paper to do." I was using Fabian tactics.

"Just for a short time. We're in Kensington now and going on to a party later."

I felt that Sarah was in the red kiosk along side of him, prodding and gesticulating and probably thinking, "It must be tonight. I'm free tonight. I must see how these inordinately strange American friends of Derek's live. See their flat on Palace Gate, the zenith of urbane life, and hear about the Shangri-La from whence they came. After all, aren't I going to America, soon?"

"All right, Derek. Make it about 8:30."

I was curious to see Sarah, too. I could change my velvet slacks for a cocktail skirt in that time. There is no chaos in enchantment.

I awoke my spouse and told him that Derek was bringing over his "going to the States on an art grant" girl friend and we were to provide orientation. I then put on a red and black burlap skirt designed by Howard Greer to bewitch, and tidied up the flat which didn't need much tidying up because I'm a quasi-perfectionist.

Promptly at 8:30 Derek and Sarah descended the staircase to our sunken habitat. Sarah did not resemble the artistic Sarah I had associated with Derek. She was young and had a certain vivacity. But unless her sizable proboscis came under the blade of a plastic surgeon, she would never appeal to my esthetic senses. Derek followed her stern and made an abortive attempt at introductions. Sarah, in her anxiety to assay the flat, had rushed into the hall and beyond Zach and I, and was examining minutely some French street scenes I had executed. Derek turned mauve in the face and called her back for the necessary introductions. Her last name still eludes me, although I have ready access to it. She had a seascape in the fall exhibit of the Royal College and I still have the catalogue. It is a name culled from the English countryside. Her father, in fact, had been a British officer lost in the recent war. Her mother, however, had managed to preserve a small house in Bushey Heath, provide a good middle-class school for Sarah, and maintain illusions of eminence. Derek had told me he did not find Mama and her illusions compatible and that there was always friction between them.

Sarah rushed around, displaying her vivacity. She tried the Hardoy, the Hans Knoll day bed, and stroked the ponderous and decorative multi-colored necklace that had come from the Chelsea pottery factory. We trailed after her not knowing quite how to respond to her squeals of awe at some contemporary design that had not entered her realm.

I was about to suggest that she might try the Japanese theatrical masks hanging on a screen, and saw a terribly embarrassed Derek. So instead, I asked Sarah what she was drinking, intimating that we had a well-stocked bar. I also told her that the bamboo bar furniture was not on loan from the Beachcomber.

"But didn't Derek tell you I don't take alcohol? I think it shows weakness."

As a matter of fact Derek had said very little about her. I began to wonder what had put this appendage around his thorax. I felt like saying go to hell but sweetly said, "How about an orange squash?"

"Lovely."

The rest of us had settled for scotch and soda and

Zach went to the bar.

Sarah had stopped flitting about and was finally roosting her diaphragm on the day bed next to Derek. I felt an odd tenseness in my entrails.

"And there," said Sarah, indicating a wall with a group of my abstract paintings. "You must have done all of these. I think you're saying something that someone else wants you to say."

Throughout the evening I was overlooking her gaucheries of speech much as one overlooks a tedious child who keeps wetting on the floor when a friend has brought "it" to visit. And underlying all my reactions a green-eyed monster seemed to be crawling. I thought, jealousy is usually in a closed chamber with desire. Zach had reentered the room with our drinks, and Derek was admiring the Danish glasses from the Strogel. It was up to me to propose a toast.

"Well, here's to weakness!" I had begun to be a bitch. I didn't subscribe to the idea of this female going off into the South Kensington night with Derek: thigh pressing him in the taxi, clinging to him all the way to his mews cottage in Putney Heath, and rushing into his damp room that reeked of turpentine, briar pipes and masculinity. I could see her bending to light the gas fire and letting the cadmium yellow flame play on her exposed, narrow, breasts. And then when it was over, lying on his lumpy mattress, sipping an orange squash, demanding an eiderdown over her languorous, short legs in repayment for this moment of treason in the dark. She is unworthy, so unworthy of him. At least, Derek, you could give me a more worthy adversary.

They had not forgotten about the party they had been going on to, and, at Sarah's instigation, departed shortly after midnight. I imagine she always had a schedule and her mental time clock was never far away. "We will allow thirty minutes for love, ten minutes for biological functions. What's that? Oh, you may have a cigarette if you like Derek. I'm for sleep. Seven hours. I have a window display in Knightsbridge at 10am tomorrow."

I lay insomniously in the ventricles of the night. The

alcohol has stimulated me. No. Sarah has stimulated me. No. Derek. No, it was the discussion. Let me sleep, alcohol. Let me sleep, Sarah. Let me sleep, Derek. Look how serenely Zach sleeps. I haven't moved an inch in the past hour, mustn't let Zach know I'm not sleeping. Zach and I, side by side, long into the night like something I remembered seeing in the Cairo Museum, on a sarcophagus, Amenophis III, and his Queen, atrophied. Was our wedlock to become atrophied? I hoped never.

There was a scurrying in the courtyard, someone had intruded on my reflections. The energetic caretaker transporting fuel to the hot water boiler. No heat, but scalding hot water for the bath. Soon, the 49 bus would begin to turtle along Kensington High Street. The park attendant would share Kensington Gardens with the London denizens by throwing open the handsome, antiquated, wrought-iron, portals at Queens Gate. Wispy haired chars would be seen with their buckets of raw sienna water, expunging yesterday's defilement of tile floored apartment entrances. Now, Zach would want his coffee and sausage roll.

Chapter Seven

"Bright eyes, what the hell are you doing all dressed up this early in the morning?"

"Zach, I'm going with you to Russell Square to-day. I won't be much in the way. I'll lose myself in the stacks of the British Reading Room until lunchtime. You will take me to lunch, won't you?" I had to escape from my lethal thoughts of the past eight hours.

"Of course, I will. I'll pick you up at noon."

That day I met Bradley Peyton the Third. Zach was generous and took us all to lunch at La Belle Meunier which was within walking distance. La Belle Meunier was one of Petronella's treasures featuring a Provencal cuisine and a remarkable cellar. But Peyton the Third interested me more. Need I say he reeked of Old Virginia in his well cut, well groomed, and well brushed clothes. With his square face, protuberant eyes and a faint smile blotted with freckles, he oozed chivalry. A buoyant and extravagant snob, son of a retired Virginia judge, Bradley would have liked to spend his own life in retirement. He was also studying international law and had reluctantly chosen London University over Oxford and Cambridge because his family maintained a flat in the West End. A product of the University of Virginia he would enjoy going back for homecoming, lingering on the spacious veranda of the Theta Delta Chi chapter house, talking to the new pledges, and getting "beery" in the blue blazer with the university crest. Here was a pinnacle of urban success who would perform well in Petronella's circus. I must introduce him to the coterie. The bottle of Merlot imported from France ordered by Zach encouraged rhetoric and Bradley Peyton proved to be an efficacious orator.

"Now, you all listen to me! Next week I'm having an open house and I want you to come by. It's time you met Wendy, too. You know where I live. Zach, you took me home in your Jaguwar one night. Gawd, that's a handsome cahr. Ahm gonna get me wahn. It's in the West End, no one is there but me. Mother and Father are in Capri."

"Yes, I know, Brad," Zach managed to say.

"You know Wendy and I met at a party at the Cloisters, that rabbit warren of flats and cockroaches. Wendy made a damn good epithet about the place," he said, chuckling mildly. "She said, 'I found the pearl in my oyster at a party in Chelsea's cloister.' Meaning me, of course."

He was now chuckling a bit more audibly, and Zach and I tried to enthuse as well.

"Thanks for the wonderful lunch, Zach. And I did enjoy meeting Gretchen. I don't know how Wendy and I happened to miss this superb establishment. Wendy's my girl guide to London. Does a magnificent job with this boorish Virginian. Wendy's really country like me, the old homestead is in Cornwall. But she was educated at Cheltenham School for young ladies." He said this with a sly grin and added, "She has traveled extensively abroad, yes extensively. You'll have things in common with her, Gretchen, she's had a fine arts background, although she's roosting behind a desk in Whitehall now. She seems to have a similar aloof way of studying people and situations like you do. Was it Whistler who said, 'Artists, like Gods, must never leave their pedestals?' Anyway you both seem to personify the bon mot."

"I'm certainly looking forward to meeting her Bradley," I interjected.

Zach had unobtrusively paid the tab to a well compensated caricature of a Victorian waiter. I had to discipline myself strictly, so as to not become hilarious as he retreated. The waiter was truly a spindle-legged, animated Ronald Searles drawing. He should have proffered us a flagon of Lemon Hart Rum on an antiquated tray with three sparkling glasses.

I think Bradley Peyton the Third would have been content to procrastinate over our coffee, but he had seen my conscientious husband glance at his chronometer.

"Zachary, is it time to go back and hit the books?"

32

Zach nodded in confirmation.

My lethal thoughts of the past eight hours again surfaced and made me speak chidingly to Bradley, "I wish you could do something with him. I have to share him night and day with that damn law library. Is such an attachment morbid or salubrious? I'm quite certain you don't do that to Wendy."

"Now, Gretchen, I know your social life together is suffering. But I wouldn't be too hard on him if I were you. I don't know if you realize it or not, but this guy with whom you share your conjugal sheets is a genius. The first genius with whom I've ever been on speaking terms. Ask anyone at Kings College."

Zach was taking it all cum grano salis.

"Excuse me for interrupting, Brad, but I have to amplify your statement a bit. Gretchen, Brad's definition of genius is a bit different than most people's. A genius to him is someone who passes the New York State Bar exam the first time around."

Brad laughed good naturedly. "Precisely. Anyhow Gretchen the fire of genius does not burn in all of us as it does in Zachary. He has different drives, different challenges. Why I imagine he spreads excerpts from Grotius and Oppenheim on his toast for breakfast."

"Unfortunately for me, you are so right," I murmured.

"On the other hand, take me for example. I was so misdirected, misinformed, I tell you. At the University, a gentleman did one of three things. He became a Doctor, a lawyer, or a Rhodes Scholar. I was told that medicine was arduous and messy, and it was difficult to get a Rhodes. Well, I'm not a compulsive obsessive about work like Zachary so the obvious thing to do was to embrace the law. At London I intend to specialize in Admiralty Law. There is not much demand for it so I will be able to relax. But," and here his voice reached a crescendo, "I was misinformed! I've met a few Rhodes Scholars over here and they are disappointing. Take Armstrong and Templeman for example." He looked at Zach who evidently would be able to pigeon hole them. "That pair of sports, they were down from Oxford last week doing their research in the local pubs. Intellectually below par, both of them." His voice reached its zenith. "Why, a Rhodes Scholar would have been the perfect niche for me."

I said to Zach, "I like him. Let's go to his open house." Rising, and displaying, what I thought was a suitable amount of reluctance, "I really must be getting back to the British Reading Room. I hear Colin Wilson is going to be there this afternoon and I'd awfully hate to miss him."

"Oh, how fortunate you are," said Brad, "I've only seen his sleeping bag on Hampstead Heath."

We were the final patrons to leave La Belle Meunier. The Ronald Searles waiter opened the door and smiled benevolently at us, exposing an inferior set of teeth in a prognathous jaw.

Chapter Eight

That night I slept better, which fact may have been attributed to the Doctor Browns Pale Ale that I had before I retired. When I awoke my thoughts were again wandering in an alien region. Was I to live under the Mango tree, regardless of the consequences? Damn Derek, his maladjustment, and his gentle, apologetic eyes. I eschewed the Royal College that day and went along to Hammersmith where the Irish Players were functioning. There, in the red light and dust of the Lyric Theatre, Sean O'Casey's "Shadow of a Gunman" beguiled me for a few hours.

Then I hailed a cab. It was rush hour and I was lucky. I was meeting Petronella for tea at Grosvenor House. "I'm an idiot," I thought for allowing only a quarter of an hour for this. The road through Hyde Park was constricted with traffic. I sat tensely, listening to the sewing machine smoothness of the taxi. Through the partially open taxi window came the sharp roar of the exhaust of one of those diminutive sports cars that frequent London, and the rich purr of a chauffeur driven homeward bound Bentley.

Petronella was engrossed in a Maison and Jardin magazine when I arrived. She smiled wanly. I didn't deserve a warm smile, I was fifteen minutes late.

"You look disconcerted, dear," she said, with her fine articulation.

"I am, Petronella. Disconcerted and depressed. I've just come from Shadow of a Gunman."

"Ah, that explains it. Never mind, the atmosphere here is so exhilarating. It will be a fine antidote for your mood. Don't you think Sir Hugh Casson has done this room in an elegant fashion? Who, but Sir Hugh, would ever have thought to coordinate this way? I'm enamored with the brass chandeliers, and that rug, a heavenly shade of green, isn't it?"

"My good man," she said to a lounge waiter passing

nearby, "will you see to our tea?"

After he had left to communicate her request to the kitchen, she faced me with consternation, and what I thought to be another new French hat.

"Gretchen, I'm the victim of anguish! Tony Carmichael is off on one of his African odysseys next month and won't be back until the opening of the grouse season."

I didn't know when the grouse season commenced, but Petronella's attitude reflected that the situation was catastrophic, so I sympathized.

"I know how you rely on Tony. Can't you prevail on him to alter his plans?"

"No, nothing will induce him to do so. Where is that waiter with our tea? The service here since the war is distressing, distressing I tell you."

As she complained, the waiter came issuing from a door nearby with the tea impedimenta.

"Oh there you are."

After the waiter had left, in a flutter of gentle chastisement, she gestured to me, "Shall I pour, dear?"

"Yes, please do. I'm still a neophyte."

"Lemon or milk, my dear. Do try one of these sandwiches. They look delicious. I am especially fond of the cucumber ones, although you may like the herring roe. Yes, I certainly will miss Tony, he dominates all my soirées. As Wilde said, the man who can dominate a London dinner party, can dominate the world. Of course, I shall entertain for him 'ere he absconds. That's what I want to talk to you about, Gretchen. It would be so amusing if you could bring along your clever art tutor whom I met at your flat last week. The one who paints portraits and has tremendous feet. You know the one I mean."

In a subdued voice I answered, "Yes, Derek."

"Also what about this flower of Southern chivalry you mentioned on the 'phone last night? I think he might do well in our little group. I like to have extra men around for exigencies. I'll let you know my definite plans next week and then you can talk to your young men about it." She said

36

this munching on a scone topped with Danish sweet butter.

One characteristic of Petronella's parties I had come to realize was a plethora of males, pseudo or otherwise.

"Quite a system of hierarchy they have here, isn't it?" I said, observing the lounge waiter direct underlings in clearing tables and straightening chairs. Another classic Grosvenor House tea was terminating. There were only two bedizened females lingering over tea. In a corner of the room a tweeded matron was scanning the Manchester Guardian.

Petronella did not seem interested in making an exodus, she obviously had nothing planned this evening.

"I'm meeting Zach at Verraswamy's at 8pm this evening. It's nearby on Regent Street. If you have nothing planned, we'd love to have you join us. Your scintillating conversation would enhance the occasion."

"How nice of you, Gretchen, I'd love to go along. Let's walk to Shepherd's Market on the way. I want to show you a charming little antique shop."

The thought of Shepherd's Market did not entrance me. The number of young ladies at doorways and on corners at this hour I always found a bit distressing. Well-dressed females, anyway mostly females, fettered to Shepherd's Market and Wardour Street, silver handled umbrellas came with hair to match. "Like to come to my flat, dearie, not an expensive venture, only six pounds. Remember this is Mayfair. Never mind the dog, bring him, I like dogs. Done kennel service before, a Great Dane once. That was twenty pounds. Of course that was for both. He could afford it. Drove a Ferrari that one. Brazen is, as brazen does."

We passed through the gauntlet unscathed, though our ears were red with embarrassment at the scathing remarks flung at us. It turned out, however, that our objective, the little antique shop, was closed.

I marveled at the fact that Petronella could always conjure up a cab when needed, as she did now, to take us to Veeraswamy's. The address was 99 Regent Street, but the entrance was on Swallow street. Petronella, maintaining her role as Ringmistress, directed our cabby. As we proceeded by way of Audley Street, she gave me a monologue about how she knew Lord Audley, his illustrious family, and his marvelous, but marvelous, glassworks. Apparently he was a frequent visitor to her flat in Belgravia.

Zach was waiting on the mezzanine as we entered. Petronella gushed thanks before we even ordered, saying she so enjoyed the food and exotic ambience and informed us this was London's most venerable Indian restaurant.

Zach had secured a table in a small alcove draped in burgundy damask with cushions to match.

As we seated ourselves, Zach announced: "I've ordered double Martinis all around. Also tandor chicken for all of us with a kind of savory coconut rice which our waiter recommended."

Petronella still gushing: "That was good of you Zach. That is my favorite Indian dish. It brings back memories. I first had it in Bombay. And then, of course, there was the Taj in the moonlight!"

I was pleased that Petronella was pleased, even though I would have ordered a good yogurt and fish curry.

While waiting to be served, Petronella delicately sipped her Martini and almost tearfully told Zach about Tony's departure for Africa and her plan for a farewell soirée.

Zach expressed appropriate commiseration and ordered another round of Martinis.

I had been admiring the décor, especially the mirrored, colorful, Indian pillows, when suddenly I had an idea.

"Petronella, wouldn't it be absolutely stunning for you to stage a Taj Mahal evening for Tony. We could all be Princes and Princesses and wear flowing saris!"

Petronella on her second Martini exclaimed, "What a capital idea! I'll do it."

I exclaimed, "Good show! I'll help you decorate."

Zach, thumping the table with his hand said, "What a romantic suggestion. Count me in. But no sari for me. I'll wear black tie and a bloody turban. It will be a memorable evening."

In a state of euphoria we caught a cab outside the Veeraswamy, which dropped Petronella at her flat and us at 19 Palace Gate.

Little did we know how memorable the Taj Mahal evening would be.

Chapter Nine

Monday morning I buttoned myself in a mature ochre suede jacket and jean skirt preparatory to going to the College. This was my less prosperous look. Zach had left the Jag which I used for transport. I was a bit tardy, because I had to find a parking place, but Professor Manfield and I now understood one another.

As I started for Studio Four and Life class, I met Derek in the lower hall, fumbling with an impossibly cluttered locker. Derek intervened. I didn't attain Studio Four.

"You're looking nice and bourgeois this morning."

That called for a glib retort, so I didn't give any. He looked absolutely beat, which opinion I voiced. "You look absolutely beat."

"Been working on my contribution to the Spring Royal Academy show all week. I am a well trained animal. I had a deadline to meet, sleeping and eating would have interfered. Want to see the end result?"

"Yes let's see the end result and I'll tell you if it was worth the deprivation. Where is this treasure?"

"It's at Putney Heath," he answered hesitantly.

I had always avoided going to his lair. This time I succumbed to the invitation. Was it just curiosity?"

"Let's go. I have the Jag. If I accelerate I can be back for the model's second pose."

I headed the Jag toward the Chelsea Embankment, top down, driving with élan, somehow guilty and excited about what I knew would happen. Under Derek's tutelage we utilized a circuitous but appealing route. Derek with a painter's vision called my attention to various phenomena in Fulham Broadway, Parsons Green, and Putney Bridge. Then we came upon Putney Heath and directly to the cul de sac where his mews cottage strived for prominence with a wealth of climbing vines. I considered it to be an excellent

40

hermitage. There were six mews cottages side by side on the street and a high stone wall confined one side of the street. Derek's was the last in the row and it had less paint and more vine than the others. Always the non-conformist. I left the Jag near the stone wall where the leather of the seats wouldn't get the full impingement of the sun. Two pints of blue topped milk encumbered the entranceway. Derek collected the milk from the cobble stones. Breathes there a mews in London whose street is not cobble stoned? With great ambidexterity, still holding the milk, he swung open his jade green door.

It was a typical mews cottage and had a nice masculine atmosphere. There was a dais in the lounge near the fireplace with a bookcase on the other side forming an asymmetrical arrangement. I visualized some expedient tenant had equipped the fireplace with gas so that a coal fire was no longer possible. The walls were a bottle green, no doubt Sarah was partial to this shade. At any rate the color formed a good backdrop for Derek's unframed paintings. There were copious still lifes, portraits, a seascape, and various drawings stacked indiscriminately about the smallish room. The only objects d'art were an unusual screen decorated with a Chinoiserie, perhaps an accouterment for our more chaste models, and two Regency chairs. A gramophone, a cracked marble coffee table, and an ample hassock completed the furniture inventory.

The path to his recent endeavor was down four steps into a narrow studio which was a shambles. On one wall stood a five by four foot canvas, quite an undertaking for a weekend. The protagonist of the painting was a beautifully executed nude, sitting on an elongated mattress. Soft, subtle, skin tones, contrasted with the coarseness of black and gray mattress ticking. An empty whisky bottle lay at her feet. It was a bizarre approach.

There is a point of no return with me and I felt it coming up. Derek started to tell me about the girl who had posed for him over the weekend and the ramifications he had when a little boy from next door climbed a ladder to peer into the window.

Then I crossed the line and burst out loudly and cynically, "You don't have to tell me what a God damned Bohemian you are! All I had to do was look at you once to know. That's a beautiful, negative, nude and I'm certain it will win a blue ribbon or whatever the hell it is they hand out at the Academy. Really, really, I think you should go in for social reform, sort of a Tennessee Williams with oil paint and brush, you know what I mean!"

Derek stood there silently facing me. For a moment I had maimed him. Even then I didn't realize there was a capacity in me for loving him. I did realize there had been a naked female sitting on this mattress in this studio not less than twelve hours ago. I would have changed places gladly. It would have been a better painting, too.

I have a more lithe form, it would have won more blue ribbons. The symmetry of my bosom is perfect, hers has a tiny mole. I have longer legs, yes and better hands. The Academy would have been sure to hang it.

"Shall we go, Derek?"

"Don't go, Gretchen. Somehow I've hurt you. I wanted your approbation so badly and somehow I've hurt you. It wasn't as you think. I paid her five shillings an hour for modeling, and that was all."

Hearing the soft, emotional words of his apology, and seeing again the picture of the nude, simple lust for him came over me.

We embraced, we disrobed, and we were on the dais. Yes, as I thought it was lumpy. A little while longer I had reached a climax more swiftly than ever before. I uttered a strange mystical cry. This is what they mean when they say loving with abandonment.

I lay there looking into his strange haunted eyes and feeling the sharpness of one shoulder bone. Sarah has felt that sharpness. Zach has heard that cry. Will I ever be able to sit on my curvaceous posterior and banter away about the merry refinements of adultery? Is it a fait accompli? Why does remorse live on? I have put a blot on the family escutcheon that I can never eradicate. No visible dividends in this black sheep. Are guilt complexes in vogue? I am singing with a sad magic. I was still clinging to him.

"Derek, you are a ducat to perdition for me."

"What did you say?"

"I said, whatever disenchantment follows, I shall never forget the magic. And now, my flair for the dramatic has worn out."

I dressed quickly, crossed the lounge into the studio, and shrouded the nude with a bit of tarpaulin I found there.

Derek had followed and stood watching me from the doorway with a denuded torso and extremities. As a concession to the skylight, which extended along part of a wall, he put on his dark corduroy pants.

"Why don't you make a good job of it?" Rapidly covering the distance between us, he threw off the tarpaulin, and slashed the canvas with a palette knife he had picked up.

"Now I'll have some coffee, Gretchen."

I ascended the steps to the lounge, the kitchen was down the hall to the right. This was the day my self-imposed discipline cracked up. I made a bad cup of coffee. Derek didn't seem to mind.

"I'm not domesticated you know."

"I never thought that was one of your attributes."

Who could doubt that at this moment we were both unstable.

Who could doubt that we were in trouble.

Chapter Ten

I ask myself why am I writing this account? I am not a novelist, I'm an artist, and there are those who question that. Always I believed one should not get out of their own bailiwick, but I have left mine and turned scribe. Consequently, this narrative will be more subjective than most. It will also not take an inflexible course. I hope you will not mind the circumlocution. I use the only tools I have on hand and, you see, I have lived for ages in a phony world. I am attempting to purge myself of him forever, an impossible feat, perhaps. I am besotted. I am impure by you Derek but maybe I helped. Together we created a maelstrom.

Thus I began to live in a charade world, playing the role of spouse at Palace Gate and concubine at Putney Heath. It was fairly uncomplicated, seeing Derek on my painting days and Zach in between his studies, the security of possessing two men. I watched myself objectively from the dress circle. I was performing well. I don't think even Petronella suspected.

Derek had renounced Sarah and when she kept ringing him up, he even got a restricted number.

"God, Gretchen, what else could I do to protect us from that shrew? I always thought only fairies and crazy bastards had restricted numbers. I realize now there are other cases."

Our aggravation with Sarah was finally resolved when she went to New York on her art scholarship.

Within me many things have become nonexistent that I once counted as undying. The memories of those first months with Derek I can say with absolute certainty have been endowed with a kind of immortality. My entire metabolism seemed to change that summer. I had always been a casual and usually late riser in the morning, take the telephone off the hook, do not disturb until eleven am, party in session last night, can't possibly play golf at nine. I don't cerebrate that early. I'm an advocate of nocturnal activities. One more Scotch, please and can't we have the Berlioz Symphonie Fantastique again?

All this changed with Derek. I would arise before Zach, sevenish, coffee, coffee, coffee. Zach would depart for the law library waving the London Times. Normally I didn't take the car to Putney Heath. I would walk briskly down to the tube station at Gloucester Road passing on the way a Lilliputian shopping center equipped with "Mac" Fisheries, Waitrose green grocery, a white-encased United Dairy, a Jardin des Gourmets, a Timothy White Chemist, an Ironmonger, and the House of Peter. Invariably I was seduced by the House of Peter. Nothing is more delectable appearing than its window at nine in the morning heaped high with rotund bath buns, butter rich scones, succulent sausage roles, dusky Bourbon balls, and above the parapet of food like a sentinel on guard was the globular face of Fat Peter himself.

I would then tube it to East Putney and perambulate past a vegetation of short streets and low roofed houses, self contained but not detached, their homogeneity broken here and there by the intrusion of an insignificant shop or some other architectural abortion. I would find Derek sleeping in inviolable solitude behind his unlocked green door.

Later, he explained, "Who the hell would want to steal a lot of conventional oil paintings these days. If I were Ben Nicholson I might lock it."

Our breakfasts were interminable. They were initiated with two crocks of coffee on the low marble table in the lounge, followed by more in the studio while dissecting Derek's work of the previous night. He had started an important portrait commissioned by a South Kensington spinster and was also laboring over a landscape of Hampstead Heath. Normally I was able to prepare breakfast without cremating any of the ingredients, while Derek read William Hickey's opinion, in the Daily Express, of literary salons, young intellectuals, and the Duke of Kent.

Bacon and French toast were beyond my skills.

Rather we feasted on what I had brought from Fat Peter's: scones, Bath buns, and sausage rolls. After the Bath buns, there was love to make. Sometimes we never got to the sausage rolls.

Happiness engulfed me. I wanted to abandon everything but Derek. I was no longer the same Gretchen Lord. I had within me the cancer of the feminine sex. I wanted to possess a youth many years younger.

"I'm too old for you, Derek."

"The hell you are."

"Just think, when you went to art school in Yorkshire, I was marrying Zach in New York."

"For Christ's sake. Where did you get all those macabre thoughts? Get up and make me a gin and bitters. No! Don't put that on. I want to look at you. It's quite a festivity, you know."

Nevertheless it worried me that I was older, and perhaps more shop worn, than Derek. Was I trying to rejuvenate my youth?

Some afternoons we would go sketching on the Heath. One afternoon we took a green bus to Hampton Court. It was serene on the grass behind the Palace that Cardinal Wolsey built. We sat there in awe just like tourists. Derek sketched an addition to the Palace made by Wren, and I cogitated on Henry the Eighth, bounder or no? A couple sitting nearby on the grass was holding hands and ogling us. They even followed us into the Garden Restaurant and kept looking at us while we had tea. I thought:were they hired by Zach to follow us? But then beautiful people were always interested in us. It was either the beard that Derek was now nurturing, or the fantastic sunglasses I had found in Soho which I wore even on dull days. We were never what one might call a conventional pair. We found ourselves laughing all through tea at a group of young boys dressed in blazers and school ties and their headmaster, who were doing Hampstead Court. The headmaster wore an apoplectic purple face caused by one called "Smithers" who kept disappearing to inspect the Royal Tennis Courts and the Maze. I'm sure the headmaster's tea time was quite kinetic.

We dropped off at the King and Eight Bells on Chelsea Embankment on the way back and sat outside looking at the Chelsea characters wandering by. We had a Guinness and a Capstan and did "cheers." Then we had a second Guinness and a second Capstan, and a second "cheers."

A venerable, blue Mercedes drew up at the saloon entrance, and disgorged three young couples. They invaded the pub in a boisterous manner, exhibitionists all, pony tails, drain pipe trousers, Italian jumpers, and lots of exuberant jargon. They paused slightly when they saw us, exhibitionists meet exhibitionists, not much room left on stage.

Fragments of their repartee drifted by and identified them as art students from somewhere in London.

"But did you see that thing Clatworthy submitted to the sculpture exhibit? It's Neolithic, I tell you! Absolutely Neolithic! I can't help it if he has exhibited in the Tate. I don't get his message."

They disappeared and we went inside, sat at the public bar, and had a third Guinness and a Capstan. A man with a bowler stood near the counter and asked politely for a St. Ivel cheese sandwich. The barmaid found one under a glass dome of sandwiches near Derek's elbow. The little man thanked her for the sandwich and drank his bitters. He was an intruder here and alone. He gazed neither left nor right, but focused his optics straight ahead on the handles of the beer taps. One of the regulars came waltzing through the public entrance with his pewter tankard raised on high and bonhomie reflected in his ruddy face. "Try a Worthington, Tom. Try a Worthington, Ken." He and his tankard had their own niche here on Friday night. On Friday night one washed the grit of London out of one's bladder with a Worthington, or for that matter one washed out the grit of London any night with a Worthington.

The King and Eight had a real confluence now, the beards, the blazers, the old school ties, the mascared eyes, were all having their Friday night out.

"Shall we go outside, Gretchen?"

"Yes, let's do."

We buffeted our way through the animated throng. "Sorry! Sorry, so Sorry." We sat down on a worn stone bench. There were faint Chelsea odors about, stale beer, petrol, urine, and a heavy layer of cigarette smog. The Thames with its moored houseboats was on one side of us, the hoary blue Mercedes on the other. The distant red, yellow, and blue lights of Battersea gave garish benediction to night traffic on the Thames. We quaffed our beer and savored the night, a casual juxtaposition which might never be repeated.

"Pubs may be making an exodus like the music-halls very soon and for similar reasons, Gretchen."

"I know, 'tis a pity."

A neat, middle aged woman standing outside peered through the window of the public bar. Soon, a man in a brown, Harris tweed jacket came out and joined her.

"Hello, Luv." Hand in hand they strolled down Cheyne Walk.

"It's been a good day, Derek."

"One of the best."

I carried away from Derek's mews cottage voluptuous memories. I put them on the tube to Gloucester Road and brought them down the stairs at Palace Gate. As soon as I saw Zach's studious shape, an ambivalence would set in and stay until morning. I had a great love for Zach, it may or may not be strong enough, against this engulfing passion for Derek. I told Derek he could never have me, and in fact didn't he have me already? Doesn't he have me still? Those were the pheno-barbitol nights and I became a dupe of neurasthenia.

Chapter Eleven

Petronella scored an overwhelming social triumph when she announced her Taj Mahal evening. She and I spent beaucoup hours transforming her Pelham Crescent flat into an exotic stage setting. I cast in plaster three Indian succubi, with exposed breasts, each with wings, about two feet in length. These brightly colored demons greeted guests salaciously as they came through the entry hall. Just as the semi-precious stones were inlaid into the white marble of the Taj to catch the glow of the moon, we encrusted the pilasters in the foyer with spurious stones and heads which glowed in our special lighting. In the drawing room, the library, and the dining room we created the three different moods of a woman said to be depicted by the Dome of the Taj, pinkish in the morning, white in the evening and golden when the moon shines. The library was the most difficult to transform as Petronella's leather bound books had to be draped in white silk made by Liberty of London and the piano festooned with white lilies. Throughout the flat we had placed numerous pillows covered with bright fabrics containing tiny mirrors. At the end, we were pleased that we had indeed fabricated an elegant "Crown Palace", truly "a teardrop on the cheek of time." The invitations were on white marble-like vellum, gilded on the edge, and embossed with a miniature Taj Mahal in gold. The week before Petronella had consulted with the chef and sou-chef at the Veeraswamy and all was in place.

The Taj Mahal evening arrived. And Petronella's assemblage to do homage to Tony was extremely colorful. All the usual ciphers were present. Petronella had chosen a golden sari set off by numerous thin, gold, bracelets on both arms. I had chosen a subdued light cerulean blue sari which I wore with silver bangles. All the men, Tony, Ian, Larry, Derek, Bradley and Zach, wore black tie and various colored turbans. The circus ran admirably in the early evening. Tony was the luminary. We were feting Tony, and Tony did a superb job in the center ring getting very little sawdust on his evening pumps. His lackey, Ian was never far from him. A slave, with a wistful visage. He was not included in Tony's trip to Africa.

Even before the festivities had gotten underway a bibulous Larry had asked jestingly, "Why don't you soar to Africa, too, Ian. Two can die as cheaply as one."

"Oh," said Ian, pretending indifference, "I don't have a Hemingway complex."

Larry picked this up and threw out, "Whatever became of Hemingway?"

Ian retorted, "Fame became of Hemingway."

"Ian, you amaze me at times. Great repartee." Tony smiled benignly from the main ring, a performing star defers.

Ian alighted demurely on a Prussian blue settee. Probably, he was only permitted one coup a week. I observed he was inaugurating this evening and bringing on his disintegration with alcohol. The drink of his choice was scotch and soda, double all the way, then to hell with the Belgian Congo, Tony, the British Overseas Airlines and the loneliness. It was obvious he desperately wanted to go with Tony.

Tony meanwhile shifted his gaze to the foyer where an elfin Petronella stood greeting Derek who towered above her.

Tony was alerted, what new menace to his security was this? He gave him more than his usual summary scrutiny. I felt a shudder of apprehension pass through my sari clad frame. Yes, I also have one Dior gown in the closet, bartered for at Harrods, at a cost of more than one hundred pounds. Expensive, yes. Worth it, mais oui! But this was sari night. Back to my apprehension. Tony and Derek were talking vis à vis.

I learned about Tony and Ian one night Zach and I were entertained at a posh party at Tony's Belgravia utopia attended by his theatrical friends. Tony and Ian wore matching tartan smoking jackets. I picked up a book on

Rome from the library and quickly put it back when I saw the enigmatic inscription, "Easter, 1953, to Tony, with love, Ian." I also remembered the studied conversational gambits Tony and Ian employed with me at one cocktail party.

"You look devastating in that azure sheath, Gretchen. Stand just a bit nearer the ivory fireplace mantle. Ah, there, like a Sargent composition, isn't she?" He would then say for the benefit of his audience, "I say, Gretchen, when are you going to divorce Zach and marry me?"

This was Ian's clue. He would materialize suddenly. "Don't be a fool Tony, we have it all planned. Gretchen's going to divorce Zach and marry me!" The lab findings were also underscored by the number of elegant young men who always appeared at Tony's parties. I was nervous that Derek would catch Tony's eye and equally nervous that Derek would unintentionally reveal something about us. Either would be a disaster.

Derek was moving into the arena on the arm of a beaming Petronella. Yes, he was playing his part well, and Tony, well Tony was definitely interested. Later, as I danced with Derek, I warned him about Tony and told him we were between Scylla and Charybdis.

Our dance didn't last long. Someone with juvenile tendencies was tugging on my long straight locks. I turned slowly and confirmed my belief that it was Larry.

"Hi, Larry, is that a Scotch for me?"

"Everything I have is yours, Gretchen. Shall I enumerate?"

"Don't bother. I understand we're having Gregorian chants again this evening."

"Good, it will give me more time to count perverts. Christ, have you ever seen such an accumulation of weirdos? Every time I look around, another one crawls out of the molding, and says, 'I'm Lord so and so.' Must be half of Burke's Peerage here. Now there is something different, a mixed twosome that might be able to reproduce. As a matter of fact it looks like she might be going upstream to spawn six months from now. Who are they, Gretch?"

"That's Bradley Peyton, the Third, and his fiancé, Wendy Gage. Bradley is studying law at London Univrsity. He's a friend of Zach's." I had been thinking the same thing as Larry, that Wendy was enceinte, but hadn't faith in my extra-sensory perception.

Larry, ever perspicuous, troubled me with his next remark.

"And who is that tall individual with the beard talking to Tony? The one who keeps looking at you as though you're Athena. I think I'll go tell him I'm in the queue after Zach."

I detoured his question with a question. Stress, stress, stress.

"Larry, tell me how you liked 'The Boy Friend' the other night?"

"I know it's a rave show, but I thought it was crass, but then you know I'm an iconoclast."

We listened to Petronella who was hovering near us with a small nucleus, giving a little acid test to new acquaintances. Her style featured a series of subtle interrogatories and went something like this:

"Were they as impressed as they ought to be by the recent work of Camus? Oh, not read him, but surely everyone has read him. Had they heard any Mozart at Glyndebourne this summer? And hadn't Ustinov been clever in his *Romanoff and Juliet*? Had they seen Viv and Larry? Were they seated in the Royal enclosure at Henly, away from the bourgeois? Had they dined at Rules? Wasn't it truly a connoisseur's delight? Edward the VII preferred it. Wasn't it a shame about the St. James Theatre? Had they booked for this? Had they booked for that? And was it marvelous and incredible, incredible or marvelous?"

Petronella's acid test had a purpose besides humiliating you if you stumbled through the answers. It was her way of culling out, as she called them, the non-contributors. Zach and I passed with high honors. I must admit this was due to Larry's warning of what to expect. The week before our first cocktail party at Petronella's we

52

combed the London Times, the Daily Telegraph, and sundry other sources to catalogue what was current on the London scene. We acquired a vast amount of artistic and social trivia. So much so, that near the end of her acid test, we were able to test her with our own questions about obscure contemporary cultural events. Needless to say, she failed.

As her little acid test progressed, Larry whispered in my ear, "This is so déjà vu with Petronella. I think I'm going to retch. Let's go to the bar."

The bar was in the foyer. I think the rug was less expensive here and able to better withstand alcoholic inundations. Petronella used a long, black, marble table as a bar on whose polished surfaces were reflected the images of scotch, bourbon and gin cylinders, flanked by silver buckets of ice, bitters, tonic water and club soda, etc. No bartender. Guests were left to their own discretion, there were very few who negotiated with the alcohol parsimoniously. Larry poured us doubles of Haigh and Haigh Pinch Bottle over ice. We were Americans, we didn't do cheers, it was an unwritten law.

Larry clinked his glass with mine and observed, "You know these parties at Pelham Crescent always remind me of the golden era of decadent Rome when the nobles gorged themselves on Ambrosia and drink and used a stomach pump to perform regorgement."

"I think you mean the Romans used the vomitorium. They didn't have stomach pumps, and if they did, I would still prefer the vomitorium."

"A reflection of your essentially coy nature, Gretch. How about another?" He playfully splashed more scotch in my glass and several splashes in his.

I endeavored to watch Derek in the gilt edged hall mirror. He was still chatting with Tony and Zach who had joined them. There was also a wench in the group wearing a décolleté red sari whom I didn't recognize. After the last splash, I was extremely mellow, I was emigrating to a remote part of myself. I took a malicious delight in not reciprocating Derek's languishing gazes. This may have been because I didn't want to give any signs to prying eyes of our relationship. After several abortive attempts to hold me with his eyes he gave up.

The next action I remember was removing my gold sandals to do the Charleston with Zach. We always were sensational at this, and we were bringing down the house. Then it happened.

A scream! All revelry ceased. Petronella ended the Bacchanalia as she came down the hallway from the direction of the water closet. She was clutching her throat as if under a dreadful hypnosis.

"Come quickly! It's Ian. Something horrifying has happened to him in the w.c."

Rushing to the water closet Zach and I looked into Ian's eyes of near death and darkness. He lay on the floor inertly. It was a nasty disfigurement of a skull and sanguinary stains on a white porcelain bathtub. There was an empty crystal glass, a rejected turban on the floor, together with a peculiar green vial. The green vial I remember most of all. It had a Lucretia Borgia look about it and lay near the crumpled twisted form on the yellow rug. It was my first intimation that Ian's fall was not entirely accidental. He was breathing stertoriously.

Zach rose to the occasion. "Gretchen, have Petronella call Emergency. Get Tony. Larry, keep those characters out of here. I'll do what I can to help.

From there on the evening became kaleidoscopic.

Tony went to pieces. "Oh Jesus! Oh Jesus! I can't bear it. Oh God, what can I do? Ian, Ian, How could this happen?" He sat on the commode tenderly holding Ian's head and weeping without restraint. Petronella had already dialed Emergency. There was almost immediate response and a paramedic and two orderlies arrived with a stretcher. The paramedic took one look at Ian and decided he was beyond his skills. Ian was delivered by the white arms of the orderlies to the waiting ambulance and rushed to the night staff at St. George's Hospital. A dazed Tony and a rather calm Zach found space in the ambulance.

The vertebrae of the Taj Mahal party was broken. The luminaries had left. The trip to Africa would never be made. Ian was already at the Gate of Death. Petronella's flat, which we had decorated as a tomb for a Persian princess, was now another tomb of sorts.

Two days later it was over. There wasn't much in the paper. Just the official announcement that Ian C. Richards, age 39, of Halkins Street, Belgravia and a respected London musician had died. He had been found unconscious from an overdose of drugs at a party in Pelham Crescent late Saturday night. A sealed envelope addressed to "Mr. Tony Carmichael" was found by police in his flat. At the inquest a reading of the note disclosed that Mr. Richards believed Mr. Carmichael had another friend, and was using a trip to Africa to sever his relationship with Mr. Richards. In light of these circumstances Mr. Richards stated he chose death to losing Mr. Carmichael's affections. The coroner found that death was due to barbiturate poisoning. Verdict: Suicide.

Chapter Twelve

Two weeks later I was shopping for a hat in Peter Jones when I ran into a very gaunt Tony Carmichael. I had just stepped out of the lift on the ground floor, and was rationalizing with myself about the high ransom I had paid for my hat, when I saw Tony browsing in the china department with a black shopping bag. I only mention the shopping bag because it seemed to cause him some embarrassment. I think it was a little frayed and his perfectionist nature abhorred carrying the thing. He was as always impeccably dressed. I hesitated a moment and then approached him laterally, noting the black band on his left sleeve.

"Hello Tony, you must be on a shopping spree, judging from the size of that bag."

"Why Gretchen, how nice to see you. Isn't this bag grotesque? I have a better one somewhere, but I haven't been able to locate it. Oh, let's face it. Ian isn't there anymore to tell me where things are. I'm going to try to get away this weekend and sort things out. I'd like to talk to you for awhile. Do you have anything on for lunch?"

"Actually, I don't Tony. Let's have lunch and chat right now if you like."

"Good. Do you mind walking across Sloan Square to the Antelope Tavern on Eaton Terrace? I prefer the chop house flavor to the prim atmosphere of the Peter Jones Restaurant with its uninspiring housewives from the suburbs, but I do admit the view from the top floor is exciting."

It was a fine, early, summer day to walk in Sloan Square. The mid-day sun was warm. There were flower carts, brimming with robust, myriad, colored flowers, in a bi-symmetrical arrangement, one on either side of the square. The fountain in the square was the repository for pigeons who were being fed by a mixed bag of loiterers enjoying the sun. An old woman sold newspapers and cigarettes. It was a

London idyll. The Royal Court Hotel serenely watched the quiet, dignified queue in front of the Royal Court Theatre. The length of the queue attested to the merit of *"Look Back in Anger"*, a play by one of London's Angry Young Men.

I looked at Tony and abject pain looked back. He gave me an ambiguous smile.

"Have you seen *'Look Back in Anger'* Gretchen?"

"Yes, twice, with two different casts. I think Osborne has something to say and he says it quite cleverly. Have you seen it, Tony?"

"Yes, Ian and I both enjoyed it."

We entered the Antelope, which I always regarded as one of the more venerable of London pubs, through the saloon entrance and jostled through the lunch crowd to a small room beyond the bar. Through the throng I could see a good stone fireplace, disfigured by cigarette butts, and on the low walls a scattering of prints of what appeared to be hunting scenes.

Tony seemed obsessed with the desire to talk about Ian, so I kept quiet and waited. I supposed I was going to be a temporary psychiatrist's couch. Perhaps anyone else with an understanding face in the china department of Peter Jones would have done just as well.

"Will you have a drink here, Gretchen, or shall we go up and eat?"

"Let's eat now, Tony, I'm quite famished."

We went up a narrow flight of stairs to the second floor restaurant, which fortunately was much less crowded than the bar. At Tony's request, the headwaiter endowed us with a secluded table near an Eaton Terrace window. I also remember thinking the room was charming. It was irregularly shaped and the dark wooden panels and broad planked wooden floors indicated age to me. I am constantly told we Americans don't know what age is, so I may be getting into deep waters.

"Looks like most of Chelsea would like to drink their lunch rather than eat it," Tony observed.

During the meal Tony hardly touched his food. Soon

57

after the waiter had brought the soup he began talking. At first he didn't look at me. His sleepless eyes fixed themselves on a red Austin that was backfiring on the street below.

"You must know Gretchen that I blame myself for Ian's suicide. In retrospect, I can see now that he acted strangely when he first found out that trouble on the plantation required me to go to Africa. I couldn't afford to take him on this trip, you see. I thought he understood. There were signals, but I didn't catch them. Sometimes I would walk into the music room expecting to find him practicing and he would just be sitting there before the piano brooding over the keyboard. As you know, I am the administrator of my African enterprises. The week before his suicide, I had to be in Paris on business. It turned out to be unfortunate that I had to take Peter Wellington, my accountant with me. Peter is young, quite good looking, and he also is gay. I am sure this enhanced the delusion in Ian's mind that I was rejecting him. I came back to London the night of Petronella's dinner party and went directly to Pelham Crescent from Heathrow. I had no opportunity to talk to Ian. I never did find out that Ian felt rejected by me for someone else until I read his note. Thank God, that as I held him in my arms in the w.c., he whispered my name. I pressed him to my breast and whispered, 'I love you Ian.' He smiled and pressed my hand. If he had gone without knowing that, I would have followed him.

"Tony, this is like one of Aeschylus' Greek tragedies. Don't lash yourself for this."

"It plays over and over again in my thoughts. His note was so pathetic. I was no longer fond of him. I had someone else. I was using the African trip as a pretext to sever our relationship. A pretext to sever our relationship! Mother of God! If he only knew! I've lost count of the hour, arbitrary separation of what is known as time. I no longer have regular periods of business, sleep, meals or recreation. I've become a bit of flotsam. I never owed anyone anything. I was ruthless in business. I was interested in nothing outside

58

of my self. Then Ian came along and I began to know quite late in life, what life and love were all about."

The nights without sleeping and the days without eating had weakened his self control and there was a film over his eyes. He blinked several times, and it was gone. With a large dessert spoon and a fork, he started to make gouges in his trifle.

"I'm afraid I'm boring you a bit, my dear. It must all seem very sordid and strange to you."

"Not at all, Tony, I have the greatest possible regard for your emotions. On a lesser scale than you, I've suffered in my time." And thinking of Zach and Derek, I felt like saying, "And I'm suffering like hell right now."

"You know at a time like this some of these people you've held in the highest esteem, don't seem to react with the sympathy you would normally expect. Take Petronella, tons of gorgeous flowers, but when it came to attending Ian's service, she said, 'Tony, dear, could you possibly forgive me for not coming, I have an abhorrence of crematoriums.' She has an abhorrence of anything with a tone of tragedy. She wasn't alone, however, many of our so-called friends didn't attend. I want to reiterate my thanks to you and Zach for being at the chapel at Golder's Green. It was grim, wasn't it? A handful of onlookers, and the dreadful closing of the furnace door. Then the macabre arrival of Larry in a top hat and inebriated, as Ian's wreaths were being carried out and the new cremation was about to start."

In an attempt to buoy up his spirits I said, "At any rate, you had the consolation of carrying out his final request."

"Yes, poor Ian had spelled out in his will about wanting to be cremated. I did that all right. And I put his ashes in the silver ewer on the piano he played so well. I think he would have liked that. You know, Gretchen, that Derek fellow at Petronella's was a lot like Ian."

Tony had picked up the check. He had gotten up from his temporary psychiatrist's couch. I had served my purpose.

In his usual gracious manner he escorted me to Sloan

Square and a taxi. Tony walked away with the frightening calm of a man who knows that there is no changing the unchangeable, the extinguished taper cannot be relit. But for me, all was not peaceful. I couldn't help wondering with foreboding about his reference to Derek being like Ian.

Chapter Thirteen

The next morning Zach had his coffee, coffee, coffee, early. He was doing research on his dissertation and it called for a trip to the Ashmolean Library at Cambridge University to study some artifacts which tangentially related to his hypothesis. I saw him to the lift and returned to my black hell. Rain was lightly impinging on the skylight, the day held a guarantee of peculiar gloom. I had slept nil. Tony's face fronted me again across the table at the Antelope Tavern. I heard the small thud of the morning mail being dropped through the mail slot in the outer hall. The char had begun her diurnal activities. It seemed a tremendous effort to pick up the mail, so I spurned it, and went into the lounge to drink coffee, smoke and fret. I was aroused from inertia by the persistent ringing of the 'phone. Wendy beckoned me from her flat in Bayswater to come for tea this afternoon. Because of the rain the telephone connection was inferior, so I couldn't be certain, but it seemed to me her tone was somewhat tremulous.

To me Bayswater is depressing. To-day, because of the pluvious weather, it was especially so. Wendy lived on the fourth floor of a gray block of flats. The building had a wrought iron fence, once black, but now peeling and rusting. There was the usual jumble of drain pipes and fire escapes on the outside of the structure and an ill kempt garden. The lift was not operating and I puffed up the four flights of stairs to her flat. A distraught and protuberant figure greeted me in a dressing gown. Wendy made no attempt to hide her pregnancy from me. She led me into her faded chintz bed-sitting room. Like a stage set from *"A Streetcar Named Desire"*, I observed a wilted bowl of hyacinths, the twin dial of a gas meter, an ashy fireplace, a fraternity photograph of Bradley Peyton the Third and a plethora of scent and night creams on a tarnished, yellow, dressing table. Wendy had been drinking and it wasn't tea. I ignored her discomposure.

I knew in her own good time she would confide the cause of her frustration to me. I imagined it was her pregnancy and that this would be the topic during our first drink.

"My bar is rather depleted, Gretchen. Would you like a gin and orange or a dry sherry?"

"A gin and orange would be marvelous, Wendy, just what I need to pick me up."

Wendy had the making for a drink on the coffee table and in true English fashion ice cubes were in absentia.

"Don't you have a fine view of Hyde Park and Orator's Corner?"

"Yes, at one time Mummy says there were quite elegant and pompous houses overlooking the park. But they fell into disrepair and became flats and rooming houses. She thinks the time will come when Bayswater will rehabilitate itself. She doesn't at all approve of my living here, you know. And Father is utterly appalled as well. Poor Father and his British Empire, and his class spirit. He's a retired Army Colonel and served with one of the distinguished Scottish regiments. They're both vegetating down in Cornwall. That's what I should have done, vegetated down in Cornwall."

Here it comes, I thought, before we're even finished our first drink.

"I should never have met a Bradley Peyton in Cornwall. And there I would never have been sucked down by the serpent of love. Let's face it, Gretchen, I asked you over to cry on your shoulder. I'm not being devious, you'll have to give me that."

"I don't believe a word of it Wendy. You asked me over for my scintillating conversation," I said with an attempt at levity.

"No, really, dear, things couldn't be worse. Let me tell you my situation. It's really rather basic and sordid. But isn't everything in Bayswater basic and sordid? After you hear me out, I have a favor to ask of you, a relatively small favor. Will you have a Players?"

"Thank you. Not now, maybe later."

Wendy lit her cigarette with a trembling hand. She had been smoking copiously and her ashtray was overflowing with twisted and gnarled cigarette stubs. She seemed abstracted for a moment, gazing at the wilted hyacinths, then she continued.

"It's a very conventional, yet romantic tale. Bradley Peyton and I met about a year ago. I was impressed with his new black Jaguar sedan with it's petrol tanks on both sides, with his Southern charm and fables, and of course, with his on and off hauteur. We enjoyed each other socially and we were especially compatible sexually. It seemed we could never get enough of each other. We took precautions, male and female contraceptives. But one time we didn't because I was in my period, and I became pregnant. Begetting of children never frightened me, however, begetting illegitimate ones did. I told Brad. He was thrilled about the possibility of a Bradley Peyton the Fourth. The pregnancy acted as a catalyst to our feelings for each other which changed from affection to love. We decided to marry and planned to announce our engagement next month with the ceremony shortly thereafter. I was happy. There was one deterrent I had overlooked, Mrs. Bradley Peyton the Second. When she heard about the engagement from Brad, she returned immediately to London. She worked quickly, and I guess Brad has an Oedipus complex which is stronger than his love for me. It's so horrendous. Brad won't talk to me. She says we are too young to marry and wants me to get rid of the child. Everything in me revolts against killing our child. Gretchen, what am I to do?"

She sat on the edge of the shabby divan, her face now a mask of British stoicism, with only a bit of moisture in her eyes.

What could I say to this English girl? You have nobody, you are alone, you are truly in the darkness. For with a woman's intuition I realized she could not win against Brad's parents who had probably threatened Brad with a withdrawal of their financial support. If he married, gone would be the Jaguar, and all the other pleasures of his extravagant life style.

"Wendy, I think I will have a Players now." I helped myself from the open packet on the coffee table. "Why don't you come along and have a late tea with Zach and I? I say late because Zach's at Cambridge drudging. I don't expect him back before half five. The three of us could sit down over scones and sort this thing out."

"Don't think I'm unappreciative of the gesture, dear, but I've already booked a reservation on the six-thirty to Cornwall. I must break it to the Colonel and to Mother. He will feel it in the marrow of his bones. He will sit before the hearth in his smoking jacket and lecture on moderation and chastity like Joyce's Jaunty John addressing the maidens. Mother will be devastated and I will sit quietly by like Isis. I am doing this with a certain amount of trepidation but father is impeccably wise and I, I'm so alone. Gretchen, the favor I mentioned earlier is this. Could you have Zach confront Bradley for me on the subject of abortion? Make him see how wrong it is to kill our child, so that when I return from St. Ives, Bradley may be seeing things more lucidly."

After assuring her I would, I left her. She was staring into space, her hands on her swollen belly. All was still, all was real. I felt an inexorable tugging in my throat as I made my descent down the antediluvian staircase.

Four days later I put a telephone call through to Wendy in Cornwall. Despite the usual rural interferences, Wendy's tones came to me. When I ascertained that we could talk privately, I told her that Zach had not been able to meet with Bradley. Pursuing the usual masculine line of avoidance and least resistance, Bradley had scurried back to Virginia.

Wendy's voice was deadly calm.

"Yes, Gretchen, I had a letter from him in yesterday's post. He enclosed a generous check for one thousand pounds, that is his Mother's generous check. He also enclosed some remorse, he could afford to be generous with that. I'm seeing the Doctor to-morrow. I understand killing a baby is quite a simple procedure. After that, who knows?"

I did my clumsy best to console her, but realized in her extremis she was not listening.

As I cradled the black receiver, I thought what minus moral values most men seem to have. Why does self-indulgence always seem to dictate their choice? How would Derek treat me if I left Zach? Would he marry me? Did he want children? I wasn't sure I did. Would some day the deterioration of my bony structure wither the bloom of our love?

With alacrity, I douched these thoughts. I had a problem. God, why had I nurtured it? Hedonist that I was, today I would ignore it.

Chapter Fourteen

It was Spring and the Royal College of Art was having a Ball. The theme was Primavera and it confused even some of the erudite. The ball was the progeny of Professor Mansfield whom I had come to love tenderly. It was said he had produced more bad pictures than any other two Academicians in the whole of the College. But I knew he was going to produce an outstanding Ball. While the Gods may have been niggardly in bestowing a painter's skills on Professor Mansfield, they had endowed him with an abundance of organizational talent, coupled with a flair for the dramatic.

Albert Hall was the site personally chosen by the good professor. Other London Art schools were invited to participate. Floats prepared by each school would assume the guise of Primordial Primavera, the Birth of Spring. The floats would parade around the cavernous floor of Albert Hall. Prizes would be awarded. Costumed revelers would sit in the stalls surrounding the floor, celebrating Spring in various stages of intoxication. After the parade of floats there would be a Dixie Land Jazz Band and a frenzy of dancers. I thought to myself, they may not like us, but like most of Europe, they love our music.

Flyers were prepared by all the Art Schools and distributed throughout London to Chelsea, Hampton Heath, the West End, Soho, and all the coffee houses and pubs. Professor Mansfield assured one and all it would be incomparable! No, the Chelsea Arts Ball would not rival it, neither would the Beaux Arts Ball, No! No! No!

I broached the subject with Zach at the first opportunity. He was lying before the fireplace absorbing *"Ancient Law"* by Sir Henry Maine. Only a modicum of heat came from the fire. It was March and still cold. Mrs. Tattersall, our char, had laid a formidable coal fire early in the afternoon, which now due to lack of replenishment, had dwindled to ineffectiveness.

"Zach, the Royal College is having a Spring Ball in April called Primavera."

I described the Art Schools and their floats, the costumes, and the jazz band, and the dancing.

"Are you interested, Zach?"

His next remarks devastated me.

"No, not really. As a matter of fact, Gretch, I've been wanting to talk to you about this *'Alice in Wonderland'* side of your existence. Don't you think you're running the Royal college, Derek, Mansfield, and company into the ground. My God, I hardly ever see you any more."

He paused and lit a Players. Our local tobacconist had run out of American cigarettes, and remembering Wendy, I had bought some packs of Players. I was failing my spouse in every department.

"Furthermore, if I went to their damn orgy, they'd nudge you in the ribs and whisper where did you get this clean shaven, crew cut, American? Isn't he odd, he has a white shirt, no braces, and he doesn't wear suede topped shoes. No thank you, Gretchen! I'll stay on my side of the paddock and I'd advise you to do likewise. You're losing your perspective and who knows what else with that duffle coat clan."

I must have looked confused and guilt-stricken from my cross legged position on the viridian carpet for then he added.

"Hell, don't look as though I've smashed all your little esthetic icons, child. Why don't you shed this thing called Derek?"

He was looking over me at the dying embers of coal in the fireplace. After a while as he sat in silence, his cigarette slightly seared his fingers. Moving quickly he tossed it into the fireplace.

"Gretchen, we know if you do a thing often enough, it becomes a habit. It's pretty basic. Undoubtedly, there is a psychological explanation for this affinity you have for London Bohemiaho. Do you find within yourself an artistic inadequacy and want to play vampire and drain it from the veins of artists, like Derek, at the Royal College? Do you want to talk about it?"

"No, not now, Zach," I said rather sharply. "Then you don't want to go?"

"That's right, No. I would prefer that you join me in my abstinence, Gretch. But, I know you'll go alone. I won't make an issue of it, not this time."

Then assuming a softer tone, "Gretchen, I love you. I'm willing to wait until you sort things out. Now the fire is low, and it's cocktail time. I'm taking orders."

A panoply of tension enshrouded Flat #2, 19 Palace Gate the night of the Royal College Ball. It was Friday and the aroma of Mrs. Tattersall's fish and chips, a devout Irish Catholic, seeped upstairs to assail our nostrils. Zach was frigid when I came home to get dressed for the Ball. He was dressed in his dark pin stripe vested suit and left immediately, saying he was having dinner at his club.

Zach's abrupt departure diminished my initial ardor for the Ball. I did not dress apropos to the theme, but went along in a black dress and silver Aztec jewelry to meet Derek at the Gloucester Road tube station.

Derek and I were not among the first to arrive at Albert Hall. There was a milling crowd outside its portals, the would be gate crashers. Only bona fide ticket holders were supposed to be admitted. I say bona fide because some of the more clever art students had silk-screened tickets and the guards were having a difficult time detecting the forgery. After a severe jostling, our tickets were accepted, and we gained admittance. It proved to be another feat to gain the stalls where we could watch the parade of floats. We were stopped by three students clad in Neanderthal fake furs, each with a bludgeon, and a bottle of Gordon's gin. We were permitted to pass only after partaking a swallow of gin.

Derek then saw Allen Sand propped against the wall. Allen never stood, he wasn't ever in a perpendicular position, but always at a tilt. When he played his trumpet in the jazz band his tilts became quite precarious. Allen was also from Yorkshire and lived on a houseboat in Chelsea. After a few gin and tonics and a few intermissions, Derek and Allen would revisit the tarns of Yorkshire. Their consensus, "People from the North are different from Londoners, more congenial, less artifice, fewer bores, and more direct."

At the tube station, Derek had registered disapproval of my lipstick as being too gaudy against its green tile and illumination. Although mildly annoyed at his remarks, my first destination was the w.c. to remove the offensive pigment and expose my face in its natural pallor. I left him paying homage to Allen's trumpet. There were times when Derek thrust these small barbs at me that I wanted to leave him alone forever. Alone, with his skylight, his canvas and his bleak quarters.

In the queue to the w.c. I got behind an atavistic wench with bare petal extremities and a pseudo leopard skin. There was a queue for the mirror and a queue for the four w.c.'s. The metal door of three of them kept clanging open and shut at frequent intervals. From behind the fourth closed door came a series of sounds for which regurgitate is lukewarm. It never did open while I was there.

A fake blue wig was being adjusted before the mirror in front of me. Surprise! It was being adjusted on the salient features of Sarah. Derek hadn't told me she was back from America. She had two sycophants advising her on wig adjustment. I recognized the two girls as painting students at the College dressed as Montmarte types. In class I had never regarded them as particularly lethal. I smiled at them and they smiled back. When Sarah saw the recipient of their smiles, her face lost its animation and she swivelled quickly around to face me.

"It's you! You are still hanging around with Derek, aren't you? You and he are quite a scandal. I believe even in America they call it adultery. Well, give my love to Zach. I do believe I'll look him up. He must be quite alone these days."

She flounced away with a fling of her blue locks to

her cohorts saying, "Let's go, since she came in, there's a decided stench here."

I could feel the rush of heat coming from my throat and enveloping my face. When I looked into the recently vacated mirror it was to remove lipstick from a roseate face. She was right. My relationship with Derek was a scandal and I was committing adultery. How long could I ignore it?

When I returned to the outside corridor, the parade of floats had ended and a jazz band was bewailing "Sweet Sue's" fate. Babel and confusion were rampant in all directions. There was a short cut across a large open balcony to the dance floor. It was a balcony of debauchery: drunks in semi-prone positions, lovers copulating, and men embracing. I quickened my pace as I felt someone tugging at my arm. In the faint light of the dance floor, I saw it was one of the students, known as Clumsy Gerald. No one ever called him Clumsy Gerald to his face, but the appellation stuck to him. His clumsiness stemmed from his eyes. He was myopic. I had seen him set his easel in life class practically on the model. His myopic, somewhat sinister, looking orbs were now smiling at me from his Beelzebub mask.

"Gretchen, have a drink with me," he pleaded.

"Thanks, Gerald." I took a swallow from his flask. This time, thank God, it was Scotch and not gin. Here was a temporary immunity from Sarah's words.

"You haven't seen Derek, have you Gerald?" Derek was his God.

"No, not yet. Actually, I thought he'd be with you, or not far behind."

"Well, he isn't. I suppose he'll turn up. He was with Allen." I thought to myself, he's probably with Sarah.

"Care to dance, Gretchen?"

Actually I could think of no more horrible doom than to dance with Clumsy Gerald, but I desperately wanted to see the activities of the menagerie on the dance floor, to ogle those that were making asses of themselves. There were those relaxed individuals who had shed their lavish customs for semi-nudity, there were altercations over dance partners

70

and there was also some excellent jazz dancing, especially the Charleston. In short, I wanted to see it all. I was a woman.

"I'd love to, Gerald."

Once on the dance floor, I morbidly drank in the tableau, so much of which Gerald with his myopia must be missing. He was looking straight over my shoulder, holding me rigidly, the way I'd watched him hold his pallette and brush. He never even noticed the female with the exposed 40C bosom dancing right beside us. My ingress into the Scotch was beginning to have its effect. I was a bit dazed. I kept babbling at Gerald and vaguely looking for Derek. We finally, I should say, I finally, located him chatting with Peggy Sand on the side of the dance floor. Peggy, too, was from Yorkshire. She was a girl in her mid-twenties, who had a pleasant round face and prematurely gray hair. Some claimed Allen was the cause of the hue of her hair. Whether this was so or not, it was evident that he had led her a merry chase, disappearing, reappearing, loving her wildly, doing everything with zest. Last summer he had gone off to Spain on an impulse, leaving her to fend for herself. Oozing with repentance, he came back in September and begged her to forgive him. Peggy, always the dutiful wife, gave in and joined him on a houseboat he had found in Chelsea. I think Derek felt a compassion for Peggy and her gray locks. If she were to live out her lifespan with Allen, one felt she would always live on the sidelines of Allen's universe. Life would not offer her many trinkets.

"Hi, Peggy, how are the Silver Vaults these days?" Peggy worked for an antique dealer in the Silver Vaults.

"I haven't sold anything in days, Gretchen. That's always the way in Winter when the tourists are gone. But Spring is here, and Summer is not far behind. They will be back. I'm so glad you found us. Derek's been frantic, thought some lecherous male had kidnapped you."

Derek came over to me. We began dancing. Clumsy Gerald sat down on a metal chair near Peggy. Derek and I did not talk. We just moved in unison. Derek was a fine

71

dancer, almost as good as I. He finally spoke.

"Don't you think this ball is terribly primordial?"

"I don't know. I hadn't thought too much about it," I said ambiguously. "I was thinking, 'If I were now to die, 'twere now to be most happy.'" I was assuming my most theatrical voice.

"You must be enjoying yourself, Gretch, when you start spouting Shakespeare at me. What have you and Clumsy Gerald been up to?"

The question was rhetorical. A tenderness came into his eyes. He was holding me very closely, pressing me to him and kissing me behind a fluted column; he was actually hurting me. The lights in Albert Hall were muted, and nobody noticed our indiscretion.

Derek murmured in my ear, "Desire is tugging at me subterraneously. I want to go away from this Saturnalia and make unrestrained, corrupt love to you."

Our embrace was interrupted by an obstreperous twosome that had sought us out behind the column. It was Sarah, looking extremely unchaste, shrilly directing invectives at me. She was with a youth from the Textile School who had one arm around her waist, and the other hand cupping her partially exposed breast. The blue wig was askew.

I heard her say, "Jesus, Derek, that's an obscene little harpy you have with you. Take my advice, get rid of the bitch before she destroys you."

Before she could say more and before I could reciprocate her defilement, Derek pulled me off to the other side of the Hall.

"I've never seen Sarah drunk before," he murmured. "Fact is, I've never seen her take a drink."

It was intermission. The jazz band was off the podium. In its place four young men with striped blazers and straw boaters were creating cacophony with an old London favorite:

"Oranges and lemons say the Bells of St. Clements."

72

"You owe me five farthings say the Bells of St. Martins."

Professor Mansfield came up to Derek.

"Derek, this is marvelous! Incredible! Incredible! Marvelous! I can turn a deaf ear and a blind eye just so long. In this case, retreat is the better part of valor. Please take over."

With that, he made his exit through a nearby corridor.

"When will you pay me, say the Bells of Old Bailey."

"When I am rich, say the Bells of Shoreitch."

We went outside to get some air. Some time later Peggy found us there. She was distraught and refused a drink. Allen had gone berserk and she needed our help to take him home. Inside the jazz band was back on the podium doing variations of "The Saint." Allen, sheathed only in a jockstrap, was doing a solo on his trumpet. He was at one of his precarious tilts, and his naked torso was bathed in sweat, which gleamed in the garish blue spotlight. Those who were able to stand or sit partook in the ritual by beating their hands or feet uproariously.

"Do you see what I mean?" wailed Peggy.

"He's not as bad as that night in Hammersmith," remarked Derek.

"The reticent English at play," said I.

After an interminable time of persuasion, Derek succeeded in dislodging Allen from his audience and bundled him in someone's unclaimed trench coat. The Primavera Ball was still very much in the dynamite stage as we made a meandering exodus. The last thing I remembered was a wizened little man with such a luxuriant growth of hair it completely subverted his face. In the center of the dance floor he was bellowing discordantly, "Girls line up on one side and boys line up on the other side. Then girls pull your pants down." I didn't wait to see what happened next.

We had gained the colony of houseboats on the Thames off the Chelsea embankment. Derek and Peggy piloted Allen in the moonlight across a heaving causeway of narrow planks linking the boats.

"A little pernicious, but so inexpensive," Peggy made a verbal toss to me over her shoulder. "The mooring costs just one pound a week. No rates to pay."

Once on board the rather picturesque house boat, we sat in a lurching, creaking drawing room just seven feet by twelve feet, drinking red wine.

Peggy continued, "We have a telephone, electricity, bottled gas, and, of course, the river is so romantic. But we do have leaks on the roof, so much so, that sometimes we don't have enough drip pans."

Allen shed his torpor momentarily to say in a slurred voice, "Woman, I don't want to hear you complaining. You know, Dorothy Tutin used to live on a houseboat here, a B.B.C. producer, also lotsa stage folk, too." The torpor then returned.

We left Peggy and Allen in their nautical drawing room and went out into the glutinous darkness that mantled the Thames. We made our precarious way shoreward.

As I looked at the evenings events, I remembered what Zach had said about sucking the blood of London Bohemiaho. Maybe it was unhealthy blood, but it was such interesting blood! But Sarah's words kept ringing in my ears. I was committing adultery! I consoled myself with the thought that these days, at least, it was fashionable.

Chapter Fifteen

I was regarding my English egg cup and the beautiful soft boiled egg which capped it. A pink ceramic cup which I had bought in the reject bin at Pegasus the day before. Pegasus will need an explanation. 'Tis a small Chelsea pottery shop catering to faddists located on Sydney Street and filled with the most unusual and unique wares. Its symbol, of course, a Pegasus-type horse. The bright motes of the morning sun shown on a lustrous pink egg cup. Surely this is a breakfast accouterment utilized mostly by the English, an important factor in the pantry of a salmon brick council flat in Paddington or a white lime and marble luxury town house in Park Lane. I sat drowsily addressing this intermediary between me and the soft boiled egg. I glanced at my watch. It lacked only a few minutes before eleven o'clock. Last night I had worked assiduously on a painting until early morn, ergo I'd slept late. The atmosphere seemed soporific in my studio with the April sun streaming from the skylight.

There was a proper time for sleep. It was a necessary ritual. But I never was able to apportion it correctly. There were too many competitors. Painting, cocktail parties, teas, theater, love, baths, and various frivolities always were in the way. Sleep, even at best, never came easily, nor did I ever remain in darkness very long. I did enjoy, however, the somnolent yawning and the luxurious stretching of waking up. Two cups of black coffee, and begone the filaments of sleep.

It was a fortnight since the Primavera Ball at Albert Hall for which I was still in monumental disfavor with Zach. To-day would be a day when the Gods altered the status quo of my relationship with Derek. The sea never stands still and the tides of change pressed forward and added a new act to the play in which Zach, Derek and I were the protagonists.

The day began innocently enough. Mrs. Tattersall

came brightly, briskly, sharply, into the room. She had been done with sleep for some time. The eternal suggestion of a smile touched her rather concave face as she brushed a wisp of gray hair from her forehead. She had been in another part of the flat and had just interrupted her cleaning activities.

"The Posts only just come, Madam, there is a letter from Gibralter for you."

She deposited the mail on the breakfast table between the pink egg cup and the butter dish. I thanked her and she returned to her cleaning. When I heard the troll of the Hoover in the outer room, I directed myself to the mail on the table. The letter from Gibralter was from Wendy. It told in a few simple sentences of a hastily arranged visit to her brother in Gibralter where she was recuperating from the illness she had in London. Soon she would be back in her office in Whitehall. Could she see me then?

The sunshine streaking through the skylight on the pink egg cup lost some of its luster. Recuperating from her illness! Poor Wendy. Having it done in Gibralter where no one would know her shame. A thwarted Materfamilias? There were big tears welling under my eyelids and trickling down my flushed cheeks. Were they for Wendy, myself or womankind in general? Wasn't I, too, a thwarted Materfamilias? If I had had progeny, I would have never entered Derek's realm. Even Zach had never known about his sterility at first. It wasn't until he went through an embarrassing series of tests that they found that his sperm count was too low. Adoption? Maybe we should have encouraged Wendy to have her baby. Well, it was still an option. Another option would be to go with Derek and quietly breed in a Yorkshire hamlet. But what would life be like in a Yorkshire hamlet? Why hadn't I been more acquisitive with my small inheritance? Why? Because I had never learned to live with conservatism. I sipped at the last dregs of my coffee and visualized a Gretchen without a car, coming down High Street in a Yorkshire village, loaded with groceries, and with two small boys tugging at her arm. The children would not wear public school hats. There would be no Nanny, no servants, and no theater in London. Could my love for Derek flourish on the proscenium I had set for it? Was it love, or an existentialist fling, and I really loved Zach? Would my life be better lived with an affection of the mild and steady order? At any rate, shouldn't I ask Derek to have his sperm tested?

Later that day the tides of change swirled and altered the status quo. It was Saturday and the day was pleasant. Derek asked me to meet him at the open market at Portobello Road to barter for a silver chatelaine which I felt I needed. Zach was again putting in time on his dissertation.

Portobello Market was inveterate. Each Saturday this inert byway burst into frenzied animation. Verily, from out of the backwaters of London as if by incantation there appeared myriad rows of barrows on each curbside. Barrows, trifling and titanic, major-domed by a competent individual, who in Cockney or foreign-flavored English hawked the merits of bits and pieces of antique ware, spurious or authentic. The contemporary was anathema to Portobello. Free enterprise and Caveat Emptor flourished with a commingling of bonhomie.

As I emerged into daylight at Nottingham Gate Tube Station from the soot-blackened depths of the unimaginative, impersonal underground, I spied Derek silhouetted against a red telephone kiosk. He had forsaken his survey of humanity for a small book which he scanned with a slight frown. His clothes, a hounds tooth jacket and dark trousers, were slightly rumpled, yet he wore them well on his gaunt frame. I knew before I was within vision range, that his shoes would need polishing, there would be a crust of oil paint under his finger nails, and his beard needed a trim. Little things which never failed to arouse a protective instinct within me.

Derek seemed to be dwelling in the core of solitude, or did he have me mesmerized into thinking that without me he was in the core of solitude? Many times he had said until I came, loneliness was the marrow of his existence. But, I had argued, isn't creativity synonymous with seclusion? He admitted it was, to an extent, but not to the extent he experienced it. To him, loneliness had pilfered confidence, belief and joy, which were also essential to superior painting.

The warm English sunshine, ephemeral in April, fructified the pleasurable excitement that was Derek's and mine from continuous discovery of each other.

We strolled unabashedly, observing amateur appearing canvases in a small art shop, a triumvirate of antique shops italicizing Nottingham Gate's competition to sell the curios of a bygone age.

Once we paused to witness the antics of a London busker doing a soft shoe and singing in the middle of the road and traffic. He played a nondescript string instrument and wore a tattered black tailed coat. A decrepit top hat added a touch of elegance.

"Incoherent music from an incoherent personality," said Derek, with a quick wink.

We moved on through the throng and turned up a cobblestone street, walking in the narrow road behind another contingent also headed for the open market.

The approach to it through the leveling of time was now a chasm of old stone house fronts, misted with a patina by the grime of countless coal fires, that issued from the innumerable chimney pots, which dotted the roof tops. On Saturdays a simple dignity graced its environs. A dignity that emanated from the gamut of antiques displayed in the street barrows flanked against uneven curbstones.

They seemed to give simple praise to what once was, arrogant and strident extravagance, leavened with a Rabelaisian lust for life.

The first few barrows we passed had brassware, coal buckets in brass, fire screens in brass, plates in brass, bed warmers in brass, new brass, old brass. The faces crowded around the barrows were young faces and old faces. One young face asked the price of a coal bucket, received an answer, paid the price and moved on. An old face who had asked and been told the price of a brass plate, negotiated with the vendor for a lesser price.   .

We passed the brass and came upon another set of

barrows, one of which particularly intrigued Derek. It held a mixed bag of old silverware, bracelets and rings, books, and a plaster likeness of David Garrick. A wispy, gypsy-like woman with a high soprano voice was in attendance. She was pawing through the jewelry with tobacco stained fingers to find something for a customer. Derek picked up the replica of Mr. Garrick, and, to better scrutinize it, wiped the dust away with his handkerchief.

"A good, strong face, Gretchen," he said, holding it in a position for me to see it well.

"He must have been a remarkable person, Derek. I'd actually like to know more about him."

"A bit of a lad, I suppose. That would have been quite an era with boys like Boswell running about in the Haymarket. In Boswell's journal I read that overnight he went along to Drury Lane to see Garrick play King Lear. His reputation was so high that even after a long run the pit and the rest of the theater was full at four, although the play did not begin until half six. Boswell went on to say that he was fully moved and shed an abundance of tears. Yes, Garrick was a talented man in a prolific time."

"Aren't we sounding like Miniver Cheevy?"

Derek gave a noncommittal grunt. He obviously hadn't read the poem. My chiding remark had gone astray.

Derek restored Mr. Garrick to his niche and smiled at the gypsy-like creature who, having scented a sale, glanced at him inquiringly. He shook his head in disavowal.

We trekked down the hill and were captivated by a series of displays inside a large arcade housing many different kinds of shops. It was here with what my English friends called typical American opportunism, I located a handsome Georgian chatelaine in a booth featuring, among other things, a Georgian baby rattle like Petronella's. After some polite haggling, one should haggle on Portobello Road, finally, there was a mutually acceptable offer.

With elation I tenderly stowed the chatelaine in my purse.

We fell into an easy cadence, shedding the romance

of Portobello Road and eventually came to Bayswater, whose shops had no splash and were just as drab and dingy as ever.

"Let's get out of here, Gretchen. The day is so lovely, how about going down by the river and visiting the Prospect of Witby? All good American tourists like the Prospect of Witby. You can't refuse me."

I agreed immediately and we entered the next tube station which was Lancaster Gate. We had walked a good distance in Bayswater. We stood in the jammed tube to Wapping.

The Prospect of Witby is one of the oldest riverside pubs in London and had been a favorite of Samuel Johnson. While it had found favor with American tourists, according to Derek, it had not yet been ruined, probably because it is a long way from the center of London and its location was in the dock area, a rather unsavory and unwholesome district. It was still, however, a fashionable haunt of contemporary Londoners and an excellent place to watch the Oxford-Cambridge boat race.

We walked from the station at Wapping over a rutted road amidst rundown row houses, children playing in the street, and garbage and refuse strewn about. Soon, begrimed tall factories with a plethora of broken windows rose on either side of the road hiding the degradation of the people's lot. A turquoise MG sports car careened past us as we approached the pub and a band of street urchins came raggedly forward.

"Watch your car, Guv?" shouted one blatantly at the MG driver.

Another left the pack and came scampering up to Derek.

"Give me a fag, Guv, and I'll entertain you with a jig."

He had annexed himself to Derek's coat sleeve and was tugging persistently.

"Ah, come on Guv, you'll never miss a fag or two. B'limey it's windy out here. Maybe you could stand me a half pint, too."

Derek flipped the urchin, who appeared to be about nine years old, a newly minted half crown, telling him to forget about the half pint and go have a lemon squash. The boy's eyes opened to a remarkable depth and shone with a brilliance that matched that of the half crown. He trotted off to display his acquisition to the other street gamins.

The Prospect of Witby sat on the bank of the Thames which it had dominated for more than a century.

Entering the pub, we encountered an elbow locked, boisterous, articulate segment of humanity enjoying the warm sunshine. It was a group that dared one not to be merry. In the Prospect of Witby this Saturday afternoon the banner of gaiety, synthetic or otherwise, prevailed. Derek requested two pints of bitters at the long wooden bar. It was surmounted by an iron grate which would be dropped at ten-thirty this evening to the accompaniment of "Time, Ladies and Gents, Time." We then chose a worn bench in a corner, a small cul de sac, where there was less group singing. As it always happens, good things end, and our sanctuary was invaded. We were in the crowd, no longer alone. So with another pint we went out to the terrace and sat on a stone wall.

There we heard the sonority of the great river boats and as our optics adjusted to the vesper light we discerned them more clearly. Monarchs of the river, stealing stealthily through the turgid water. The gusts from the river played with my long hair. I was extremely exhilarated. I had invincible strength. I could always walk the continent of night. In that precious moment life had great peril for me.

Derek's sotto voce brought me back to the terrace of the Witby.

"You look good that way. Rumpled, windswept and unstudied."

Derek wasn't prodigal with his compliments, and I was pleased.

Now, adopting a serious mien, Derek was heading the conversation adroitly in a new direction. A direction I

81

hadn't foreseen.

"Gretchen, I've had an offer, a fairly good offer, that is, to go out and cultivate the Fine Arts in Africa. You smile, and you have every right to smile, it probably sounds like an appropriate place for plying my trade."

I said nothing. I didn't want to hear what was coming. He continued.

"Actually, I'll be head of the Fine Arts Department at Makarare College in Uganda. There is no problem with the language. Uganda is still a British protectorate. I understand that in about 1962 it will become part of the Commonwealth. And Head of a Department means a considerable salary. I understand there is a magnificent view of Lake Victoria. Could I interest you in Lake Victoria or in leopard hunting, maybe? You know I want you to marry me and go with me. I won't go alone."

The moment of decision that I had hoped to eschew was imminent. My mind seethed with convolutions. The ineluctable pull of Africa. It tugged at me. But who was this Derek? What are his constituents? How had I permitted him to develop in the dark room of my heart? Was the negative overexposed?

"Don't be an ass, Derek, of course you could go without me. Aren't you forgetting about my conjugal appendage?"

Derek didn't answer and, evasively, I found myself questioning him.

"Are they giving you any time for decision?"

"Three months."

"Then I, too, will have time for a decision."

"Just three months. I see, you can't tell me tonight, Gretchen, that you'll chuck it all and go to Africa with me? I can't blame you either, you know. I'm afraid in the end you would regret me, my bucolic beginnings, my mannerisms, and my inferiority complex. With me, you wouldn't have your after dinner brandy, the Jag, and the Dress Circle would have to go. Life with me wouldn't be the life you have been used to."

"Are you withdrawing your safari offer?"

"No, I just want you to realize the inferior standard of living you would have with me."

Striving for time to collect myself, I said, "You've told me about the starkness of life in the North Country, now tell me of its beauties."

"Agreed. One day I will take you North, north to Haworth as a start. We will go into the hills, valleys and hamlets together. We will visit Wordsworth's shrine, Milton's roosting place and Ruskin's on the opposite side of Windsmere. Perhaps we will see Campbell in his racer from the top of 'Old Man's', a mere mote dancing on Coniston. I will show you red and gray mountains, ochre fields, terre verte trees, Bronte land, a miner's path near Wath on Derne molded by heavy, steel-capped boots and a row of derelict terrace houses, now shells, of stone with black apertures for windows. Yes, there is a type of beauty in the North Country, but it is a raw beauty that needs the surgeon's scalpel to lay it bare."

Emotionally, he continued.

"Do you know how drab and countless the moments are when you're not there, Gretchen? Of course you don't. I never tell you. Well, I dwell in an ugly void. I flounder. I am equivocal, adrift, an abstraction. A bloke not there at all."

Derek's monologue had given me some time for reflections, and I continued.

"Derek, by going to Africa, won't you be stifling your painting career? I think so. Perhaps you should remain here where there are opportunities for your work to be recognized?"

"I haven't had much success. I don't seem to get any recognition. At least in Africa I could support you in a decent lifestyle."

"If you are considering Africa seriously, you should talk to Tony. He has business there and knows it well. Also Tony is well connected in the art world. As you know, many of the critics and Gallery Directors have a similar sexual orientation as Tony's."

Derek smiled equivocally. "Gretchen, all I know is that before meeting you I lived a homogenous, bucolic existence, a few paintings, a few women and a few holidays."

"Do you realize how your life has deteriorated? While you still have a few paintings, you only have one woman and no holidays."

"I like moving down this wonderful incline," he said, putting his partially full beer mug on the wall nearby and gently kissing my forehead.

Simultaneously, our adopted urchin materialized and drained his mug of the amber liquid with a gulp and whispered, "Thanks, Guv."

We exited the Prospect of Witby.

Yes, the tides of change had swirled. The status quo had been changed.

Chapter Sixteen

Coming home from the Prospect of Witby, I felt a kinship with Shakespeare's tragedies. All mortals have individual choice and the play moves forward, shaped by the stimuli of the actions of the players. Up until now, I had been in charge. Derek was responding to my passions. Zach was immersed in his studies and so far was playing a neutral role. My little charade was going well. I was secure. There was no need to make a decision now. Derek was impoverished. I had no resources to support a permanent union. Put it all on the back burner. Now Derek's role had changed. The teaching post in Uganda would enable him to support us. He was forcing a decision.

Then, Zach's role changed, too.

I was in my studio carrying on a conversation with a gouache. Whatever else might be my faults, I was outstanding with color. Although living in New York, I was a charter member of the Washington Color School and had exhibited in the Jefferson Place Gallery with Ken Noland and others. That kind of color had not been introduced in the Royal College. Rather, they were fond of timid, washed out, thinly applied, muted color. I prepared the glass slab with vivid hues and the colors talked to me. I was an anomaly to the English.

The best they could say was, "Well, they do it differently in America."

Zach appeared in the doorway. Usually at this time he was in Russell Square.

"Care for tea with me? Take a break. I've asked Mrs. Tattersall to prepare us a high tea."

"Love it."

I climbed down from my stool and rushed off to deal with the smudges on my hands.

There was peace in the flat. It was familiar and comfortable.

Zach sat in the Hardoy chair. On the long, ebony table was Mrs. Tattersall's formulae for high tea: kippers, scones, gooseberry jam and an assortment of small, delicate sandwiches.

The door of the lounge was slightly ajar. I could see Mrs. Tattersall preparing to depart.

"Goodnight, Madam."

"Goodnight, Sir."

Then, there was only a glint of illumination at the edge of the door, an elongated optic from a Dali world watching us.

Zach was striving to communicate with me. I could feel this. I'll try to make this facile for him, I thought.

I buttered a scone studiedly and smiled at him.

"I have some news," he blurted. "I've done what I think is best for us. I've booked our passage on the Muaritania for next month. I've almost completed my research here and the University has granted me permission to complete my dissertation in New York."

Contrasting this with his earlier enthusiasm to complete the degree abroad, I realized it was a tribute to Zach's high moral code that he was obliquely telling me to make a decision about Derek. Why didn't he tell me straight out? Could it be that he was afraid of losing me and chose finesse?

Tensely, he observed me, watching for a reaction.

He added, "You could wind up your classes at the Royal College in a few weeks, couldn't you, Gretchen?"

One, inhale. Two, exhale. Three, inhale. I had put my face to sleep, lest some paroxysm display my tumultuous emotions.

"Yes, Zach, I am sure it can be arranged."

"Good. I'll contact the estate agent and see about the lease. You'd better tell Petronella. She'll want to give a going away party. Oh, by the way. That Derek thing. It's your call. But remember, Gretchen, although we've grown apart lately, I will always love you. And I think down deep you really love me."

When I looked up, he had gone.

How quickly the focus had changed. I could no longer relegate it to the back burner. I must keep calm. May I not tomorrow retrogress to where I was yesterday? I can choose any life I desire, providing I know what I desire.

I saw Derek the next day at the College.

He greeted me with a smile and we had elevenses in the common room.

"Gretchen, I followed your advice. I called Tony and told him about the Africa offer. He was very interested and asked me to have lunch with him next week. He also wants to see my paintings. We seem to have a repartée."

"That's good, Derek. He is very influential. But be careful with him."

"Oh, I see what you mean. You know they are also here at the College. That's probably why I haven't progressed."

I wasn't really listening. I had to inoculate Derek. I quickly told him about Zach's transatlantic plans.

Derek's reaction was immediate and masculine.

"Surely, you're not returning with him. You must go to Africa with me! We complement each other. Your angle of vision is so utterly different than Zach's."

"I'm uncertain, Derek. I'm in the throes of a frightening dilemma."

He looked at me closely. In his face there was a soft, sensitive, look.

"Gretchen, you can't go. I won't have it!"

That night a hydra-headed fear seized me. I was suffering from a vaso-motor disturbance, undulating hot and chill flashes seized me. This passed and I fell into an agitated slumber.

I dreamed that Zach and I were at Henley on the Thames. We had come up for the Regatta in the Jaguar with the top down. There were acres of very white tents and bright hued pennants lifting to the winds. Near the shore hilarious punt loads of spectators drifted in holiday attire. My blue organdy dress and large straw hat fluttered in the breeze.

A burnt sienna punt pulled into shore and a girl with a green dress and a slight curvature of the spine stood up to disembark. A man with a yellow blazer helped her ashore. She was clumsy, the punt rocked perilously as she stepped out. Her green parasol spattered on the surface of the water, followed by hoots of laughter. The man with the yellow blazer retrieved it.

I stood watching a group of blazers, Mauve, red, black and blue with white flannels and rowing caps.

"Aren't they garish, Zach?"

"Gretchen, don't talk so loudly, they'll hear you."

Zach took me by the hand and lead me off as though I was a recalcitrant child.

A gaily-bedecked band played, two small boys passed us, eating flossy candy cotton while drinking orange squash, which reminded me I was thirsty.

We passed a blue and white stand selling drinks and ice. There was a queue, a very orderly queue. Some people in the queue sat on newspapers on the grass, awaiting their turn.

"May I have an ice or a cool drink, Zach?"

"Not just now, darling."

A young man, very thin, sitting on a shooting stick, clad in a navy blazer and a straw boater overheard us. He had a short black beard.

"May I buy her an ice? I don't mind the queue."

"Thank you, No," Zach said stonily.

The band ceased playing. The racing shells darted back and forth on the mobile July water. The public address system announced the winner of the last race in a rasping tone. The oarsmen cheered. The nice young man gazed through binoculars.

Zach now had me in a vise-like grip and was saying, "That chap is a plebian, Gretchen, watching the regatta from the banks of the river. We must watch it from the veranda of the Steward's Enclosure in our own milieu."

I looked back, the plebian man with the shooting

stick disappeared.

I stopped to read a sign, "Competitors Amenities Tent." How British, I thought.

There was a tug on my hand, I stumbled and fell. When I got up, my powder blue dress was stained. Oh well, no one would notice it.

We ran madly on looking for the Enclosure. I had begun to feel extremely thirsty again, my armpits were drenched with perspiration.

Abruptly, Zach relinquished my hand. Why?

I looked up. The Steward's Enclosure was directly ahead. A gargantuan sign indicated the approach. Zach stood talking to the uniformed man at the gate, they were far away.

The heat was unbearable. I was squinting and I could hardly see, amoeba danced before my eyes in naphthal red and alizarin crimson. I opened my purse and took out some pink harlequin sun glasses. I put them on and people began to stare at me.

I felt a gentle touch on my shoulder and turned about. It was the nice young man holding out to me a blue ice. It just matched my dress. He proffered the ice to me, smiling with a kind, handsome smile. He was ever so tall. I reciprocated his smile and started to reach for the ice. Zach slapped my hand and hurried me off to the Enclosure.

I turned about to regard the young man once more. I recognized him now. He was Derek. He began to shrink and wither like a Chinese litchi nut.

Zach said, "Gretchen, I love you and now you can have an ice. Any special flavor?"

I awoke, choking with tears.

I was incredibly tired and I wanted to abandon Derek to Putney Heath, Zach to the Mauretania and myself to my psyche. I couldn't sleep. How like Lady Chatterly, I thought. The gamekeeper had put me at hazard. Forfeit Derek! But not my protector Zach.

Chapter Seventeen

The next day I decided to visit the new exhibit at the Royal Academy. I had to be alone. For me, I had always found solace in places like London's National Gallery and the Louvre, in Paris. Each was a separate world of its own. Their collections of paintings and sculpture soothed me and comforted me. No Derek. No Zach. Perhaps in the massive marble halls of the Academy I could sort things out. When I closed my eyes, the dramatic, surreal events of my dream were italicized.

I rode upstairs on the No. 9 bus with the smokers and the usual assortment of dogs as far as Piccadilly. I noted in transit a crowd in Hyde Park, a trickling of visitors to Wellington's home, a new model Jaguar convertible in Henley's window, and an exotic fruit display at Fortnum and Mason. I still remembered in Wellington's home the unusual painting showing only the backs of Napoleon and Wellington as they were viewing the battle scenes.

I went solitarily up the steps to the arch leading to the entrance of the gray stone Academy, watching the flags fluttering capriciously atop. I paid my 2 shillings, 6 pence at the turnstile and bought a catalogue. To enjoy the Academy, it is said, is a sign of advancing years. If so, I would have a "go" at senility, because I really enjoyed the Academy. The Summer Exhibit was colossal, of course, approximately 1,500 items, both good, bad and indifferent. On this point Sickert said the last word in 1910, "You can not fill fifteen galleries with masterpieces."

I passed over the prints in Gallery VI and the etchings in Gallery IX and sought out some of the works mentioned in reviews of the Exhibit by the London media.

In one Gallery there was Annigoni's concept of the Duke of Edinburgh, and the late John Minton's "Composition, 1957," a Camino Real type of study on a theme of James Dean's fatal car crash, full of carrion and disaster signals. Nearby was a John Bratby wickerwork style Trumpeter who appeared to be drinking a high C out of an almost drained trumpet.

The cynosure of the Exhibit was the controversial 750 pound sculpture of Churchill by Ruskin Spear. Critical remarks emanated around it as from no other work: "Disgusting!" "An appalling caricature!" "A great white blob on the landscape!"

I continued on, viewing Gallery after Gallery.

How are decisions of the heart made? Surely not by an analytical process of marshaling facts and categorizing them, pro and con. So much for Derek. So much for Zach. The winner to be decided not by the preponderance of the evidence, but rather beyond doubt!

Suddenly, my being fused into oneness. My spirit soared. It came over me like a flash of lightning. I realized I still loved Zach. I always had loved him. True, I had an affection for Derek and he excited me sexually, but it wasn't love. Zach was my love, my life. I don't know what happened to me. I remembered, "Lead us not into temptation." I had yielded to temptation. Is life a highway with tempting side roads enticing the morally weak? Zach loved me still. He understood my sin. Our love would transcend my transgression.

I had to see Zach. I bolted from the Academy, past the abortive Sir Winston, the lorgnettes, the Carol Weights, the raw umber and the rose madder, past the information counter with its battlement of post card reproductions, flung down my catalogue, and came to grips with the exit turnstile. I was free, absolutely free; already I was jubilating. Everyone must know I was exhilarated, the somber attendant at the exit smiled at me.

Out into the vortex that was Piccadilly. I was alive. God had been good to me. I was bedazzled by the traffic and bustle. No number 9 bus for me. I hailed a taxi. Yes, Zach was my life. Derek had shrunk and withered like the Chinese Litchi nut.

Giddily, I left the taxi at Kensington High Street and

went down Palace Gate feeling that it was beginning to be enameled with bright sunshine. The Devore Hotel was host to a newly painted gray façade, balconies were pregnant with blooming plants, flat windows were raised in nearby Thorney Court. Inhaling love, I turned into 19 Palace Gate.

Zach, as usual, was sitting in the Hardoy chair with an open legal tome before him.

I rushed to him and threw my arms about him.

"I love you darling, only you."

I started to explain about Derek.

Zach stopped me short, saying, "Gretchen, I don't want to hear about it. I have you back and that's all I want. Q.E.D."

That night Zach and I slept together and the passion I had thought gone had only been dormant. My orgasm was swift and multiple. Zach, as he always did, waited for me. Finally, he raised himself on his elbows and appraised my nudity, my erect nipples, my flat umbilicus, protuberant hips, my lithe, lean body, an exercise in angular joints for life students.

"Gretchen, you're amazing. I thought I'd lost you forever."

He took my face between his hands and admitted me into his eyes, infinitely deep orbs, stroking my hair.

I began to weep. My strength left me. The play was back to status quo. I was no longer a cosmic exile floating in a void.

Chapter Eighteen

I slept soundly. My arms around Zach. All was well. I'd call Derek today.

The telephone rang. Zach stirred himself to answer it. He came back.

"It was your Aunt Stella's attorney. She's in Mt. Sinai hospital asking for you. A stroke, I'm afraid."

Aunt Stella, loyal Aunt Stella, who had been my only Mother.

"Zach, we must go right away!"

"There's no need for grave clothes yet, darling," he said gently.

I felt nothing, my sensory equipment had gone dead. Visions of the antediluvian Franklin, the antimacassars on the stiff upholstered chairs in the Music room, the monstrous Grandfather clock chiming in the hallway besought me.

Zach came rushing back to the bedroom.

"Success, Gretchen; B.O.A.C. has two cancellations on the eight o'clock plane out tonight. Pack up. We can make it."

I was in a state of shock. I kept going back to the Mohawk Valley and those happy days with Aunt Stella.

"May I have a Scotch and soda?"

"Permission granted, but just one; we have much to do."

I gulped at it, murmuring, "I'll just throw a toothbrush and a few clothes in a suitcase." I wanted to ring Derek and tell him about Zach.

Zach had packed his own bag. He was good at that.

"Comes from my Army training," he'd always say. "I also shine the backs of my shoes."

The clock was ticking. We'd have to leave for Heathrow soon. I thrust open bureau drawers and heaved a sheaf of lingerie and assorted outer garments indiscriminately into a traveling case.

I went into the hall and dialed Putney 1969. There was a Brup, Brup, Brup. It rang but no one answered. Well, bad news could keep.

I returned to the bedroom and resumed my helter skelter packing. I heard Zach ringing for a cab to take us to the airport. It would be here soon.

I left a generous check for Mrs. Tattersall to tide her over until our return. I told her I would let her know our New York address if anyone wanted to contact us. I also had time to call Petronella, who had been very fond of Aunt Stella. Petronella asked to be kept in touch. She also mentioned she had seen my art friend Derek lunching with Tony. They seemed to be enjoying themselves. I didn't get it, then.

Upon arrival in New York we called Mt. Sinai and found that my Aunt Stella had expired quietly while we were over the Atlantic. We were able to get a room at the Plaza. We always enjoyed being near Central Park. I called Petronella immediately. She was devastated. I also called Mrs. Tattersall.

The next few days we were engaged in preparing an obituary for the New York Times and the upstate papers. Aunt Stella wanted to be buried in the family plot at Cazenovia Lake where my mother and father were buried. I arranged for the funeral service to be held at the nearby Catholic Church, St. Luke's, which she attended. I had the reception afterward at her venerable Victorian home, which I found that I now owned. I also found time to write Derek, but the letter came back stamped, "No Such Addressee."

While nothing was ever said while my Aunt was alive, we both knew I would be her heiress. She would say, "Now Dear, you must learn how to take care of my Chippendale dining set and the Wedgewood." Yes, I would inherit the Victorian mansion, its contents and the Franklin. And along with it a substantial fortune. Aunt Stella was not a proliferate spender and her gilt-edged investments had kept growing.

It took almost six months to settle Aunt Stella's estate and we were now into February. It was a relief to finally be able to pay some attention to our own affairs. Zach had continued the rent at 19 Palace Gate. Mrs. Tattersall was still taking care of it. The Jaguar was in storage.

Now, it was time to return to London.

Petronella met us at Heathrow in her Rolls. She took us to 19 Palace Gate. As she dropped us off she said, "Why don't you come with me tonight. Tony is having a reception at the Marlboro Gallery for that young artist, Derek, who moved in and replaced Ian. I understand Tony arranged an exhibit for him at this posh Gallery in Mayfair. I think you knew him at the Royal College of Art. May I pick you up later?"

Zach and I looked at one another. We both now knew why my letter had been returned.

We thanked Petronella and accepted. She said she would pick us up at 8pm. We were greeted by Mrs. Tattersall, who beamingly said that she had prepared a high tea and the kippers were especially good.

Zach made a fire in the hearth to subdue the dampness in the flat. It was good to be back again. The Marlboro Gallery receptions were always fascinating and we were curious to see Tony and Derek as an item.

Petronella's chauffeur gave up trying to find a parking place. There were Rolls, Mercedes, Armstrong Sidleys, Rovers and a host of smaller cars taking up every available space. We were dropped off at the brightly lit façade of the Gallery and Petronella asked that we be picked up in an hour, as we planned to dine at the Dorchester.

The Marlboro was extremely crowded with the stylish and chic, the systemized spirit of posh London at work. I found out Tony had sent gilt edged invitations to most of Belgravia's and Kensington's matrons and to all of his acquaintances in the art and antiquarian spheres. I wondered if it was pay back time.

The doorman greeted us ceremoniously as an effluvia of rich perfumes and wine drifted toward us. Near the entrance of the salon, Tony and Derek, dressed in black tie with red carnations adorning their lapels, were welcoming a host of admirers. Petronella said she didn't wait in queues. We slipped by and had a glass of champagne proffered by an attentive serving maid. Six of the paintings displayed were portraitures, the rest were canvases which Derek had at Putney Heath. The portraits had been done in the past six months while we were away. Quite an accomplishment, but then, he always painted with celerity.

The largest was a life size painting of Tony in evening clothes. It was reminiscent of Whistler's portrait of Auguste Duran. I remembered advising Derek to talk to Tony about Africa and mentioning to him Tony's influence in the art world. Given Tony's dejection on losing Ian and Derek's obsession with his negative self-image of his life in Yorkshire, it wasn't difficult to see that they filled a mutual need. For Tony, Derek replaced Ian. For Derek, Tony was his entry into the Royal Academy and a world of wealth he had only dreamed about. For me, I was happy with Zach.

The other portraits were of eminent friends of Tony's. They included Lord Audley of the glassworks, Sir Charles Wheeler, C.B.E., P.R.A., Dr. G. B. Dowling, and Sir James Gunn. Of all of them, Tony's image had the best light and positioning. Complementing it was a large bowl containing a cluster of purple-lipped irises in the center of a Louis Treize table.

By this time, Tony and Derek were circulating through the Gallery. Tony came up and kissed Petronella and myself. Tony was ecstatic and received our accolades by saying, "It is a wonderful portrait and it gives me great pleasure." He then quoted Oscar Wilde, "Pleasure is the only thing worth having a theory about. Beautiful things, like beautiful sins, are the privilege of the rich." Kissing Petronella again, he dashed off, seeking another glass of Champagne.

Petronella remarked, "What a difference six months makes. I doubted he would ever recover from Ian. I was expecting Tony to reenact the demise of Petronious, you know, the Arbiter Elegantiae. Tony always had a flair. But he seems quite happy now. I can't say the same for his friend, Derek. He should be excited and pleased with this evening, but he's not."

Derek walked stonily by us as we departed for the sanity and the elegance of the Dorchester.

Epilogue

On the morrow, the critics' reviews of Derek's show were uneven. The best was that his portraits were adequate, but his landscapes superb. The worst was that his portraits were too thin and lacked body, but his landscapes were adequate. At any rate, I found out from Petronella that all the portraits and two of the landscapes had sold. Tony had praised his protégé to her and was gratified with the exhibit. Apparently, also pleased, was the Marlboro Gallery, which had promised Derek another show.

I saw Derek one more time. There wasn't much to say. When he had lunch with Tony to discuss his African offer, Tony pointed out that going there would mean utter stagnation for his hopes of a painting career. Tony asked to see his work and Derek had taken him to the Putney Heath mews. After looking over his canvases, Tony told him if he stayed in London, Tony could get him several commissions for portraits of important people and an exhibition at the prestigious Marlboro Gallery. He offered to let Derek live with him in Belgravia while he painted.

Derek felt I was repelled by his boorish Yorkshire manners and really didn't want to leave Zach. I was simply having a frolic. Tony was offering him everything he had ever wanted and Derek was willing to pay the price. He was now Ian's successor. I told him he was right. I loved Zach and would never leave him. I think this made him feel more comfortable with his decision. Over the years, Derek became a very good painter and was accepted into the Royal Academy. Petronella wrote me from time to time and Tony and Derek continued to be an item. I was happy for both of them.

While in London I contacted Wendy, in Cornwall. She came to London and had tea with Zach and me at the Connaught Hotel. I was delighted when she offered to pour. Tea is so ceremonious. We had a lovely chat. Wendy was engaged to a boyfriend from her childhood days and matrimony was eminent. She was very content and promised to visit us in New York with her spouse.

As for Bradley Peyton the Third, we encountered him lunching alone at The Algonquin in New York one day. He was practicing real estate law in Stanton, Virginia and living with his mother. We didn't talk about Wendy.

Zach, now Dr. Lord, is a professor at Columbia University Law School, teaching Jurisprudence in the English tradition.

I have continued my painting and last year had a vernaissage at a prominent New York gallery. The critics called it "...an outstanding explosion of color and harmony... a must see show."

We enjoy our fast-lane life in the Village and weekends in Westport, Connecticut. In the summer, we are at Aunt Stella's mansion in upper New York State, which I have preserved as she wanted it.

Truly, the tides of change ebb and flow. Individuals make choices. Each choice by an actor in the play affects the choice of another actor. Would Derek have met Tony if he had not met me? Did Ian's choice to die open Tony's world to Derek?

Did my adultery with Derek help me finally to acknowledge to myself the great love I have for Zach?